SERIAL

A NOVEL BY

G.Lusby

Ocean View

Serial

G. Lusby

Copyright ©2009 by G. Lusby
All rights reserved. No part of this book may be reproduced in any form or by any electronic or mechanical means, including information storage and retrieval systems, without the prior written permission of the author Gary L. Lusby, except by a reviewer who may quote brief passages in a review to be printed in a newspaper, magazine or journal.

First printing June 2009

This is a work of fiction. All of the characters, names, and events portrayed in this book are either products of the author's imagination or are used fictitiously. Any similarity to real persons, living or dead, is coincidental and not intended by the author.

Printed in the United States of America

ISBN: 978-0-557-06892-0

GL *Publications*
Ocean View
www.lulu.com/GLusbyBooks

Printed by Lulu Enterprises
Morrisville, NC

1

Jennifer pushed the key in the lock and swung open the door. She slowly stepped in, closed the door, and reached for the light switch. Her hand massaged the wall, searching for the switch as if someone had moved it. Finally finding it, she flicked the switch but nothing happened, no lights.

"Damn, must be a power failure from the storm," she said as she looked around, waiting for her eyes to adjust to the darkness. Why does this have to happen the week that the rest of the family is vacationing at the ocean and I'm stuck here working for a living?

In the still of the darkness there was a creak; a small noise in the distance that pierced the silence like a bolt of lightning. She froze. Her heart began to pound as she felt the adrenalin pumping in her body. It's nothing, she told herself. Still she paused and waited; waiting for that god awful second sound or the wonderful sound of silence in the night. Nothing. Should she leave out the front door and go to her neighbors or investigate the problem herself. It's twelve-thirty at night; surely she wouldn't disturb her neighbors for nothing.

She fumbled in her purse for a tiny keychain flashlight she always carried; hoping after all this time the batteries would still be good. I just have to clean this purse out someday, she thought, as the fumbling continued. Finally she found it. She turned the tiny gold tube and a small beam of light cut through the hallway darkness. A tiny sigh of relief expelled from her body as she turned and glanced back out the front entrance window to see if any lights were on at her neighbors but none were visible. Well it is twelve-forty-five at night, she thought, as she shined the light on her watch. Who would be up at this hour on a work night?

She walked slowly down the hallway towards the kitchen to see if all the lights were out. Flicking the kitchen switch, nothing happened.

Darn, now I have to go down the basement to the circuit breaker box.

She turned just as another creak echoed through the hallway. She twisted and quickly shined the light down the hallway towards the front door. Good, nothing in sight. Were these the normal sounds of the night that ordinarily she pays no attention to? Maybe, but still her breathing quivered as her heart pounded. This is silly, she thought, I'm heading downstairs.

She slowly began walking towards the downstairs door. As she passed the living room entrance she again stopped, feeling as though she was not alone. As she started to move the light towards the living room her nightmare came true. Faster than she could react, an arm was around her neck and a hand was over her mouth. The flashlight fell to the floor rolling the beam of light into the darkness of the living room. She struggled to break free, struggled to scream her lungs out, struggled to kick this person who had her locked against his body. She could feel by his strength it was a man, and feel the stubble of his beard or mustache scratching her cheek. His breath was hitting the side of her face.

"Don't say a word, don't scream, don't fight me, or you will not live to see the light of day."

The words rang in her ears as she relaxed her struggle. Involuntary tears were filling her eyes as only breathing filled the silence of the house. This can't be happening, this is a bad dream.

She was forced to her knees as he quickly taped her mouth shut with duct tape, then her eyes. She was forced to the floor and in doing so managed to strike him repeatedly with her failing arms. He straddled her body and forced her arms over her head taping them together. She lay motionless wondering what was to happen to her...will I live. God, please don't let him kill me!

His breathing was heavy and not a word was muttered. Needless to say her heart was in her throat waiting and waiting. She could hear him doing something but since he had stood up she couldn't tell what. She prayed to herself, please be a robbery...if I could only tell him to take everything I own, just please don't hurt me.

Suddenly he was kneeling next to her as he slowly began to unbutton her blouse.

Oh God, he's going to rape me, she thought to herself. She involuntarily swallowed as tears began to drain from her watery eyes. I don't want to get raped, but if it will save my life, then do it and get it over with.

As he finished unbuttoning, he pulled her blouse out from her skirt and opened it fully, then ripped open her bra, removed her skirt, then panties. She could feel his hot breath as he began to caress her breasts, and then his mouth was on them.

Oh God, please help me.

He positioned himself on her as he tried to force her legs open and leaning close to her ear whispered, "We can make this easy, or we can make this very, very hard, it's up to you."

I just want this to be over, she thought, and gave him no resistance. His hands forced her legs open wide, then even wider, as she thought she didn't know her legs could open that wide.

She could hear his heavy breathing and sensed he was just staring at her as the coldness of the rubber gloves he was wearing began to caress each part of her body. Suddenly he stopped and before she knew it was on top of her as she felt the brutal pain of him slowly pushing inside of her. She could sense he wanted to savor every moment as he ever so slowly forced himself all the way in. He was gentle, not overbearing like the animal she thought he would be, but he went on and on and on. It hurt terribly, he just seemed so large compared to the only person she had ever been with, Randy her boyfriend. Randy was always so gentle.

It seemed like forever but he finally finished and was off of her. She didn't feel anything inside of her so she knew he was wearing a condom.

She sensed he was standing up dressing himself, and then shivered as he knelt down beside her again. His mouth was next to her ear as he whispered, "Thank you sweetheart, I've wanted you for so long. You have a wonderful body; now, goodnight beautiful!"

She could sense a certain familiarity in his voice, but the panic inside overcame her thought process as he again straddled her body. Suddenly his hand was over her taped mouth as he pinched her nose shut.

Oh God, help me.

She began to kick and roll furiously, but his body was too heavy. Her breathing became heavy as she felt the tape partially come off the corner of her mouth forcing air out of her tired body. He slapped his other hand over the tape as she quickly tried to suck for new air. She began to get light-headed as the struggle for more air weakened her body, her head spinning as her mind became dark and confused.

Her life seemed to flash before her as hundreds of thoughts raced through her mind. I'll never see my parents, my brother, and my boyfriend Randy again. Streaks of light mingled with the darkness as she wondered what will happen to me before it is all over. Who will rescue me, how will I be saved, when will I wake up from this horrible nightmare? Who would possibly do this to me, someone I knew, a stranger in the night? Why isn't my daddy saving me? Why isn't Randy pulling this jerk off of me?

The streaks of light got brighter now as her struggling body relaxed. It was over, she couldn't compete with him.

2

Jennifer Connelly was a likeable nineteen-year-old blue-eyed blonde with a beautiful face, accentuated by a beautiful bright smile. Growing up in the town of Forest Lakes, everyone knew her as a sweet, fun-loving, hometown girl that every parent would love to have and every boy lived to date.

She had decided to forgo college with her friends and take a teller job at the local bank, waiting until next year to head back to school. After twelve years of public school she needed a break from it all and besides, she wanted to just have some fun for a while, socializing with her friends and making some real hard-earned cash.

She lived with her parents and younger brother in the same house since they were born; the same house where she babysat her brother when he was a toddler, had her girlfriends over for sleepovers, and gave out her first kiss to Bobby Hickok on the front porch when they were thirteen years old. She loved this house. It was perfect. It was home.

Her boyfriend of four years was her high school sweetheart, Randy Bigby, who lived about two miles away. Sometimes they would each start walking and meet halfway just to say hello, steal a kiss, and then head back home. One evening last week they did that three straight times in a row, until her Dad told her to do something useful like helping her brother pack for their vacation.

Her brother Jack is fourteen, a great kid, but with a wicked streak of laziness running through him, not to mention the streak of sloppiness that continually surrounds him. He is just starting his first year of high school and is scared to death thinking about going to a new school. Even though he already knows a lot of people going, it's still a scary experience thinking about being in school with the big kids. Jack was pretty much the kind of kid who stayed to himself, not that he was a loner, just that he was pretty shy and to himself.

Her parents, Todd and Elizabeth, are both in their early to mid-forties and have lived in Maryland all of their life. The rest of their family is here and they love being close to both their parents and siblings, and the Maryland climate which gives them a firm taste of all four seasons throughout the year.

Every year the family heads to Ocean City for a week, but this year Jennifer was working and couldn't get off since she hadn't asked in time and figured she needed the money anyway. The whole family really looked forward to the week away since it was one of the few times they were all together for a reasonable amount of time. The past four years they had been allowed to take a friend with them on the trip which made it really neat having someone their age to bum around with, walking the boardwalk and tanning on the beach.

Jennifer and Randy had tons of friends, mostly the old high school crowd. All the guys played sports together in high school while most of the girls stayed close to them through cheerleading. Most of the crowd was going to the local college, so they lived at home, like her. Her best friends were Fran Thomas and Roxanne Willowby, both nineteen, and both excited about college, college boys, and the newfound freedom of graduating from high school and tackling the real world.

Their crowd hung out either down at the local park or at the local sub shop which was a crowded little shop with hoards of regular customers who loved the fantastic subs and pizza. Booths ran down one side of the shop and that's where you could usually find two or three of her friends. The local park, which was only about a block around in size, was also a popular place especially in the spring and summer. Located in the center was a small pond usually loaded with local ducks and an occasional flock of geese who were there hoping to be fed by the many families that visited the park for spring and summer picnics. Picnic tables lined the grove of trees surrounding the pond, so it was a popular spot to just take in the view on a beautiful breezy day, which is why Jennifer and her friends liked this place so much; it was a great spot to pull two picnic tables together, gather around, and just hang out together.

On this bright sunny day in May, little did her friends or family know of the tragedy awaiting them?

The Connelly's arrived home from the ocean finding it difficult to find a parking place. The call had been placed Friday morning that there was a problem at home and they needed to come back immediately so they did the three hour drive in record time. As soon as they saw the flashing lights from the multitude of police cars their biggest fears took hold...the thoughts of a burglary were suddenly cast aside; too many cops, too many somber neighbors. Their entire house, yard, driveway, and street were encircled in yellow tape marked *Do Not Cross*. They pulled their car off to the side as close as they could and the three of them got out and were immediately approached by local police who questioned their intentions, then led them under the tape and over to a superior officer.

They were greeted by Lieutenant Tim Franklin of the local police department homicide unit, and told what had happened the night before.

Tears of disbelief filled their eyes as they came to grips with the horrifying tragedy. Why did this happen and who could have done such a thing to their only daughter, their little girl. They were led into the house where they both collapsed to the couch as the somber news rang uncontrollably through their mind sending tears streaming down their faces. As they collapsed in each other's arms the rest of the world was blocked out as they comforted each other repeatedly saying "no...no" and "why...why". Jack, her brother, couldn't bear the news and went running out of the house.

"I'll go to him," said Jennifer's mom, as she tried to get up off the family room couch but almost lost her balance as the lieutenant grabbed her arm to steady her.

"No, I'll go," said her husband, "you just sit down and let me talk to Jack. It's gonna' be real hard for him to come to grips with this...they have been so close these past few years. It's hard for all of us, but he's only fourteen. I'll go."

He walked to the front door and was directed to the garage by the policeman outside on the porch and headed straight for the side door that was hanging open. Wiping the tears from his own eyes he found Jack sitting on an old wooden trunk in the corner, sobbing.

"It's not true Dad, it's not true. Please tell them it's not true. Not Jennifer."

"I'm sorry Jack; none of us can believe what has happened. I know how close you and your sister have become in the past few years, and I know how important she is in your life, but we all need to be strong for her," his father pleaded as his own voice quivered with sorrow.

It was hard for the Connelly's, as it would be hard for any family to accept; losing a daughter is a tragedy that no family should ever have to endure.

The next few days would be very tough for them. Tough to bury your child; tough to see her life end while your life goes on; tough to realize that someone out there deprived you of the enjoyment of watching her blossom in life. Soon sorrow will be replaced by hatred!

The police crime investigation unit searched the entire area and determined that the intruder entered the house through the rear door using a glass cutter. A round hole had been cut in the bottom pane, large enough for a hand to reach through, unlock the doorknob and deadbolt, and open the door. The house and yard were completely sealed off as investigators combed every inch of the property, dusted every piece of furniture for fingerprints, every floor wiped for shoe prints, and of course her body which was photographed from every angle before it was removed.

Lieutenant Franklin, who was the lead investigator, had his team interview everyone in the neighborhood, but no one had seen or heard anything at all that night. A few neighbors had seen Jennifer leave for work in the morning, but that was the last they saw of her. The house was equipped with timers so the lights would come on at 6pm and go off at 11pm. Many neighbors noticed this happening every night, but nothing else unusual.

At the conclusion of the initial investigation, there were only two clues. At the rear door where the intruder entered, a cigarette butt was found, and no one in Jennifer's family smoked. The second clue, which the police did not release to the public, was that on Jennifer's body the attacker had left a message. Using a black magic marker, the duct tape that was on her mouth had the message *'I am so sorry'* written on it. The crime lab removed the tape, sending it to their lab for processing before anyone else viewed the body. Knowing that serial killers usually leave some kind of mark or message, they wanted to keep the message a secret. The last thing they wanted was promote the killer by advertising his or her message of sorrow.

The preliminary results of the initial investigation uncovered that the house was full of fingerprints but most of them were of course those of the family. The only other prints prevalent throughout the house were those of her boyfriend Randy whose prints were on the furniture, the doorknobs and doorways, and even glasses that were in the kitchen sink. His footprints were also outside of the house but so were Jennifer's, right alongside his.

3

For the two days following the murder, the police centered their investigation on Jennifer's friends and relatives. They not only wanted to gain all the information they could on Jennifer and her habits, but to see if they had noticed anyone suspicious around her in the past month or so.

Lieutenant Tim Franklin was married with two daughters of his own, both teenagers, so he could only imagine what the Connelly family was going through. His interrogation with them was short and to the point and left no doubt that they were not suspects in the case, he was just doing his job. He would spend most of his time with her boyfriend Randy and the bulk of the crowd that were closest with her.

The lieutenant asked Randy to gather together all their friends and he would meet them at the park in the afternoon. He wanted to address them as quickly as possible while the last few days were still fresh in their minds, so hopefully getting them together in a quiet serene place like the park would make everyone feel more comfortable under the awful circumstances.

When he arrived there were eleven of them gathered around two of the picnic tables, six girls and five guys including Randy. They looked up as he approached, except for Randy who was just staring at the ground, undoubtedly having the hardest time coming to grips with the tragedy as he was continually consoled by his friends.

Randy was a big guy, about six-foot, 245 pounds, with broad shoulders, dirty blonde hair, and the bluest eyes imaginable. His eyes were the first thing you noticed about him, they were so blue they were striking. The very first thing anyone would say upon meeting him was 'wow, you have the bluest eyes I have ever seen'. He played football through high school and was captain of the team the last two years of school while Jennifer was on the cheerleading squad making them inseparable in school and out. It seemed so out of character to see this big guy so depressed and grief-stricken, but Jennifer had been his whole life for the past four years. Their relationship often had its ups and downs due to Randy's personality traits, but since their graduation from high school two years ago they had been virtually inseparable.

Next to Randy at the table were Mike Hadley and Fran Thomas who were the closest couple to Jennifer and Randy doing just about everything together. They too had been dating for two years and were the same age, nineteen. Fran's parents were best friends with Jennifer's parents, so the two families spent quite a bit of time together socially, even occasionally vacationing together down the ocean.

Next were Margy McNichol and Peter Hamson who were the youngest couple of the crowd. They were both eighteen and had just graduated from high school this past year and had been together the longest, having gone to school together since third grade. Everyone always joked that they were meant for each other since they had been together for so long and would never be able to break up and put up with anyone new. Margy's dad and Jennifer's dad worked together in the same office downtown as marketing executives, so they often spent time at each other's house going over business related issues.

At the other table on one side were Rhonda Collins, Stephanie Hampton, and Roxanne Willowby, all friends and ex-cheerleaders from their high school days. This elite group of beautiful girls had formed an early bond in their early high school years and had been inseparable ever since. They were all so similar in their personalities except for Stephanie who was playfully known as the 'bitch' of the group. All the girls were so sweet and loving, but Stephanie was the kind of girl who was good-looking and knew it; she never let you forget how special she was; because of that, most of her male relationships were very short-lived. But the rest of the girls loved her anyway and always got a charge out of the way she handled herself, especially with the guys. They each cherished their close friendship and the 'click' of being the most attractive girls on campus. Most of the guys would kid them about being a conceded bunch of girls, but the guys lucky enough to be in this group of friends' loved spending time with them.

On the other side of the table were many of their newer friends that had joined their group within the past year or so. Billy Marshall, another 19-year-old heart-throb that all the girls loved, had just moved to the Forest Hill neighborhood the past year. He started at the college last year and immediately was taken with this group of girls. He was in Stephanie's psychology class and once he arrived in class, it only took her three days to move in on him and bring him into her fold of friends. Billy wasn't the usual jock type that they all loved, but was almost the opposite, a smallish built kid but with a great personality and a gorgeous smile that usually melted every girl he met.

Next in line was Becky Thomas, Fran's fifteen-year-old younger sister. Even though she was much younger than the others and even though she was still in high school, she was mature for her age and was probably the most beautiful girl of the group. Her long blonde hair and striking body made her a favorite with the high school guys, but Fran, as well as the guys in the crowd, kept a close protective watch over her. If anything, Becky had a hard time dating guys because her choices were usually scrutinized to death. She was the kind of girl who was so beautiful that most guys were afraid to approach her for fear they would get turned down; plus most of the guys figured she was a lot older than she was because of her looks and oh-so developed body.

Next to her was Brad Townsend, the oldest member of the neighborhood group. He was the 24-year-old in the middle of this group of 19-year-olds, and admittedly the odd-ball of the group. He wasn't a jock, he wasn't a college student, he didn't live in their immediate neighborhood, and he didn't date any of the girls in their group of friends. In fact, he was the one person in their crowd that didn't go to school with them or even grow up in their neighborhood, but he did have a hidden crush on one of the girls and would usually spend most of his time with her; that girl was Becky. He met Becky at the park about three months ago while taking his dog on a run, a dog that led him into their fold. He was playfully tossing a ball around for his dog to retrieve when the dog just about knocked Becky down chasing after it. Brad ran to her rescue and immediately fell upon her beauty. He had started his own photography business as soon as he moved to town, so beautiful things naturally attracted him. He persuaded Becky into coming to his studio and modeling for him, just as a trial, thinking maybe it would lead to some beautiful photographs and maybe a professional career for her so she spent quite a bit of time with him at his studio and he naturally met not only her parents but the rest of the crowd.

The one thing he did have in common with the crowd was his remarkable good looks, that JFK, Jr. kind of look, with dark black hair, green eyes, and a great body that he worked on continually. When he first met Becky's friends he was immediately welcomed into the group, especially by the girls who loved his looks, his body, and his charm. But being five years older than most of them, he made it known that he was interested purely in making some friends and having a good time. So sadly, the girls backed off their flirting ways but were very protective of him from any girls outside of their click. Besides photography, he loved to work out with weights and keep himself in tip-top shape. Anyway, his infatuation with Becky was totally his secret, he never voiced his feelings to anyone; Becky and he were total friends, although very close.

All eleven of them were close knit friends that usually socialized together as a group.

The lieutenant pulled up a third picnic table and stepped up on the seat, sitting on the tabletop.

"Hi guys," he said, with a solemn but strong voice.

They all echoed a simultaneous glum hello.

"Is everyone here today?" he asked.

"Yes we're all here...although a lot of our parents are a little skeptical about us talking to you," answered Roxanne, who they all called Roxy for short, although many of the guys in the crowd called her Foxy.

"Okay, I fully understand that and you can let them know that I'm not here today to ask you any questions individually. The reason I asked all of you to gather here today is not only to say I'm sorry for the loss of one of your very close friends, but to try and piece together any clues that may lead to her killer. All of you knew Jennifer inside and out and were always a part of her daily activities, so for this reason I want you to think, and think hard, about the last week or two. Remember every moment with Jennifer and every little thing that happened, as incidental as it may seem. When you go home tonight, I want each of you to start writing down anything you can think of; people she knew, places she went, incidents that happened, anything that you can remember. In a case like this, many times the smallest detail leads to the killer. So think hard and you may be the one who leads us to catch this guy."

They were all mesmerized as he talked and nodded in unison as each request was made. Tiny involuntary sobs could be heard as each of them was reminded of the tragic incident. Many of the girls had their heads lying on their boyfriends shoulder or held hands as tears replaced the usual laughter they shared when they were all together.

"Bastard!" snapped Randy as his stark blue eyes shed tears of disbelief and hatred.

"Yes, I know," said the Lieutenant as he reached over and placed a hand on Randy's shoulder, "but now is not the time to dwell on madness and hatred, now is the time to help your girlfriend by capturing this animal that ended her life. Now is the time to get this guy before he hurts someone else and before too much time passes and you forget the little details of the past week or so. If we can retrace all the details of her past week, maybe we can get this guy before he gets too far away. Help me, okay?"

"Sure," they all echoed as they glanced toward each other.

"Great," said the Lieutenant, "and I also want each of you to write down on a separate piece of paper everything you each personally did yesterday hour by hour. This is not to say I suspect any of you, her closest friends, but the law states I have to eliminate people one by one, and that includes all of you. So, thanks again, and we'll talk in a day or two. If you think of anything at all that you feel is of utmost importance, feel free to call me right away, day or night."

He hopped down off the picnic bench and one by one handed each of them one of his cards with his number on it. As they watched him walk slowly back to his car, nothing was said until his car pulled slowly out of the parking lot, spilling a cloud of dust behind it.

"I can't believe we're all suspects, we loved her," snapped Margy.

"I know," said Roxanne, "but we all need to just get over it and help get this guy as quick as we can.

Jenn would have wanted it that way. And anyway, how do they know it's a guy?"

"They must have some clue; otherwise they would have said a man or woman," said Margy.

"They know it's a guy," said Randy, "Jenn was raped."

The horrid words sent everyone tearfully into a giant hug that lasted for minutes. One by one they began to get up from the tables and slowly walk back to their cars hand in hand. The dust had settled on the road from Lieutenant Franklin's car as each of their cars began to filter out of the lot. They each had something to do, something very important to do, for Jen as their minds were racing with thoughts of the past 48 hours. They wanted her killer caught!

4

Two months would pass with no clues, no leads, and to everyone's frustration, nothing that could help the police with the investigation. Each of her friends accounted for their time by either being with each other or home asleep. They each met with the investigators several times and presented lists of Jennifer's friends and acquaintances throughout her school and social life but no one could come up with any leads as to who would want to hurt Jennifer in any way.

The investigators were at a loss; no clues from her friends, no clues from her fellow workers at the bank, and absolutely no clues at the scene of the crime. The cigarette butt, a Winston, found at the back door had no fingerprints or recoverable DNA markings, and they couldn't link the brand of cigarette to anyone who knew her. Randy and Brad were the only two members of the group that smoked and neither smoked that brand of cigarette.

The intruder obviously wore gloves during the entire act because there were no strange fingerprints anywhere inside or outside the home. Randy's fingerprints were all over the inside of the house, but as everyone said, both he and Jenn were together just about every single evening after work. The first suspicions of him were immediately dashed by his parents who were up until the wee hours of the morning talking with him in the kitchen about college.

As far as the unreported marking on the duct tape, the killer used a common permanent marker which was completely untraceable. Handwriting specialists examined the message but could do no more than record their findings for now with no suspects. Also there were no saliva markings on her body since it was evident that her entire body had been swabbed down with an alcohol solution. The trail was empty. The killer had obviously done his homework and covered all the bases when planning this premeditated murder.

The investigation continued forward with most of it centering on two of the guys in the group, Randy and Brad.

Randy was obviously the person, other than her parents, who spent the most time with her. They had always been inseparable and wanted nothing more than to be with each other constantly; other than that, he was the last one to see her alive and the last one to talk to her. He told the police she had called him from work before she left, as she did just about every day, and told him she was going to spend the night primping herself by washing her hair, doing her nails, and soaking in the tub. They agreed to have dinner the next evening. The calls were confirmed upon investigation of phone records.

Brad was the oldest and newest member of their crowd and unlike everyone else in the crowd, he was from another state. His roots and background were not planted in this community so many people immediately questioned his history; especially when it came to hanging around so often with a fifteen-year-old girl. Becky's parents admitted they were very skeptical of his intensions at first, but after visiting his studio and spending some time with him, they accepted his intentions as purely professional. Lt. Franklin still took DNA samples from both Randy and Brad and had each one give an unsuspecting sample of their handwriting by writing a message of where they were that night.

July was an especially hot month this year. The weatherman blamed it on *el nino* as they had the past year or two. A dry hard drought had plagued the whole area with all the rain coming in from the west being stopped by the Appalachian Mountains. Everyone and everything was just plain hot.

Mike and Fran, Jennifer's closest friends, always threw a huge summer party every July at Fran's house for the whole crowd. It was an annual event all through high school and usually a week or two after the Fourth, since a lot of their friends and their families went away for the holiday. Fran's parents had an in-ground pool in the back yard, so the party was always at her house. It was *the* big summer event that everyone always looked forward to.

Her dad, Bob Thomas, was a local bank executive and hired Jennifer immediately out of school for the teller job. Her dad and mom were in their late thirty's and were always active participants in their kid's activities. Most of the time Fran and her younger sister Becky would kid their father that he just wanted to be young again and part of their crowd, but he would always assure them that he had no desire to rejoin his teenage years and just wanted to be a close part of their lives; something he himself missed as a child. But when it came to his daughters, and their friends, he would always go all out to have a fantastic party for everyone, cutting no cost to make it the summer affair Fran was proud of.

All of the kids in the crowd had especially great relationships with their parents. Of course there were the occasional parents vs. teen standoffs that are prevalent in any family; but these were all good kids living in a strong middle-class neighborhood. All the parents knew each other through the many school years their kids were together and usually came to the party to spend time with the other parents. Everyone had debated not having the party this year because of what had happened, but Fran's parents had talked to Jennifer's parents and they insisted it would be the best thing for everyone. Jen would have wanted it. So the party was a go.

The hot summer night brought everyone out dressed in their skimpiest bikinis and shortest shorts. The guys were spending most of their time either in the pool or around the food; while the girls were bathing in the sun and continually trying to get the guys to dance. The barbecue grill smoked all night long filled with burgers, hot dogs, and chicken wings with sauces that were labeled *hotter than hell*.

Most of the parents that came gathered on the screened-in porch on the other side of the house to leave the kids to themselves and stay a safe distance from the music. They usually only mingled with the kids when they wanted something more to eat or the kids requested their presence. Most of the parents were a middle-aged crowd in their late 30's or early 40's, so they got along real good with the kids.

Jenn's dad was always the class-clown of the fathers and found it hard not to be intermixed with the crowd of kids, either throwing the football with the guys or parading around with his arm around the girls. He wasn't happy unless he had everyone laughing about one thing or another and it usually took Jenn's mom to finally grab him by the arm and pull him away from the crowd of kids.

Stephanie's dad was the macho dad of the group and could always be located by his black muscle shirt and dark, dark tan. He usually was always challenging the guys to a swim contest or sitting around surrounded by the girls as he told one of his harrowing adventures. It usually embarrassed the hell out of Stephanie and her mom but all the kids had known him forever and they actually looked forward to his stories and tall tales; his handsome face and physique didn't bother them either.

Fran's father was always the cook, but gracefully played the vanishing chef as he prepared the food then quickly disappeared so as not to embarrass Fran or Becky in any way.

"Dad," Fran would laughingly say, "you're not part of this crowd, go find your own place to play!"

He would laugh and just keep on bringing out more food. The rest of the crowd would always plead with her to leave him alone as he paraded around with one of her girlfriends on each arm. He was a handsome middle-aged guy and was devoted to his wife and daughters, but he loved being around Fran's girlfriends and playing the old macho role. Her friends always loved his debonair look and his outrageous sense of humor that always kept them laughing and hanging on his arms. But as much fun as he always had at the parties, he was a work-a-holic and always had an excuse to leave and tonight was no exception.

"Your mother will have to pick up where I left off because I have to slip down to the bank for a while. Now I know the party will probably dwindle down to a boring crawl once I leave, as I'm sure most of you girls will miss my handsome smiling face."

Everyone laughed as he danced his way into the house, with Fran and her mother just shaking their heads in embarrassment.

The parents lasted until about eleven or so but the kids stayed until about one in the morning when Fran informed them that the curfew hour had arrived. Most of the guys piled into their cars after their goodnight kisses and hugs, but many of the girls were spending the night as they always had. Roxy was the last to leave, after trying to help clean up everything.

"Just go," Fran insisted, as she pushed her out of the yard and over to her car. "I wish you were spending the night with the rest of us."

"I know," she said," but I'm meeting John early tomorrow morning for a big day trip we have been planning, so I want to get to bed early."

"Okay, we wouldn't want to get in the way of you and Johnny-boy...so call me tomorrow when you get back and tell me all about it," said Fran as she hugged her. Roxanne's car was the last to leave the driveway.

Fran's mom wasn't out by the pool when they returned, so her and the girls started to clean up but decided they were too tired and they would leave the mess for the next day. Truthfully she knew her and her friends would probably spend half of the remainder of the night upstairs talking about everything happening in Forest Lakes, so they would probably sleep in and her parents would be up early and take care of the mess for them. She was right. All the girls talked on and on about every guy they could think of and they even rated them all on a scale of 1 to 10. Naturally most of their close guy-friends topped the list...of course.

It seemed like they were asleep only minutes when the commotion downstairs woke them all. It was daylight outside, so they had been sound asleep for much longer than it had seemed. It sounded like yelling and screaming at first, but as Fran jumped up and opened the bedroom door she could tell it was more pounding and crying than anything. As she ran downstairs most of the other girls had also awakened and were following behind very hesitatingly; Dad and Mom don't usually fight with each other so all the commotion seemed strange.

They were hugging each other and Mom was crying her eyes out as Fran raced down the steps and over to them. She hadn't even noticed that the front door was open and standing there were two detectives, one of which she recognized immediately as Lieutenant Franklin from Jennifer's case.

As she reached them yelling, "Mom what's wrong, what's wrong!" her mom came over and threw her arms around her. Tears were rolling down her face and Fran could hardly understand her for the continuous sobbing.

So her dad stepped in and said, "Honey, I hate to tell you this, but last night Roxanne was attacked on the way home."

"Attacked," Fran yelled, "by who...where is she now?"

"I'm sorry," her dad said, "she didn't make it, she's gone."

Fran was numb. She ran over to the other girls as they screamed with disbelief and grabbed each other. By this time her dad had walked over to the door and invited Lieutenant Franklin and his associate into the living room where they asked all of them to gather to discuss what had happened.

They were all a basket case as the lieutenant tried calming down their uncontrollable screaming and sobbing.

"Please girls, calm down so we can talk...I'm so sorry, but please try to calm down."

"Did the same thing happen to her that happened to Jenn," Fran shouted as she pulled her face off of Stephanie's shoulder. "What is going on, I don't understand why all of our friends are getting killed? Who is doing this...who?"

Lieutenant Franklin spent the next two hours at the house calming everyone down and explaining in detail what they assume had happened to Roxanne after she left the house last night.

Her car was spotted in the woods just past the entrance to Chesapeake State Park by a motorist passing by. The passenger side door was open wide and the inside light was on, which is what attracted the passerby to stop and see if someone needed help. Roxanne's body was laying in the backseat, completely nude with tape on her mouth, eyes, and hands, the same as Jennifer. Preliminary reports were that she too was suffocated by the killer. Since this was on her normal route home the suspicion was that she ran into someone along the road who turned out to be her assailant.

Obviously the investigators didn't tell Fran and her parents and friends all the details of the murder scene, but it was strikingly similar to Jennifer's murder in many ways. Obviously the taped mouth, eyes, and hands with the same type of duct tape, the suffocation of the victim, the rape, and above all, the telltale sign of what looked to be a serial killing; the message written in black marker on her taped mouth, 'You are so beautiful'.

Again, the murder scene was free of any fingerprints inside the car or out, and it appeared that the killer was smart enough to have taken a branch of leaves and swirled away his tracks as he left the scene; so no shoeprints or tire marks were there to suggest the assailant's size or if he was in a car. And again, no semen or DNA clues were left; her body again was cleaned with alcohol.

The coroner estimated that Roxanne had been dead approximately three hours from the time she was found. The other interesting fact was that another cigarette butt was found next to her car and this time it was another brand, not a Winston like before, it was a Salem. But regardless, it was a freshly smoked butt.

Lieutenant Franklin was terrified at the thought of this information getting out to the general public. They obviously had what seemed to be the beginnings of a serial killer on their hands and the last thing he wanted to happen was the public to go into a panic frenzy. They had to catch this guy as soon as humanly possible...but how, with almost no clues to go on. Here we had two local girls murdered within two months of each other and a community that was beginning to suspect more than just mere coincidence. The words *serial killer* would surely surface before too long.

5

The week that followed was again tragic for everyone, another funeral for a teenage girl of the community. Funerals are especially sad, but when the funeral homes are filled with teenagers, young adults and small children, it makes it an especially sad place to be.

The parents were obviously devastated and both Jennifer's parents and Fran's parents consoled each other continually at the funeral. They knew each other from graduations, school affairs, parties, and vacations, but never had they dreamed of spending time together like this. Both of the boyfriends, Randy and John, who were obviously best friends all through high school, and spent so much time together after school, were not only devastated, but mad, fit to be tied. They wanted this killer and they wanted him to answer to them, now.

Again the investigation centered on the close knit friends and their social life together. John, who wasn't at the party but had plans with Roxanne the next day, was at the local restaurant where he worked until two in the morning and arrived home within ten minutes of getting off. Most of the others in the crowd were also either home or still at Fran's house for the night and Brad was at the studio by himself although he couldn't get anyone to vouch for that. Becky had seen him earlier in the day at the studio and they had talked on the phone about ten-thirty when she called him from the party. He couldn't make the party due to a large photo job he had promised out the next day, so he had to spend the entire day and night in the studio getting the job processed and finished. He had established quite a reputation for himself with his custom pictures and albums, so most of the community used his services for special occasion pictures.

The investigation for both crimes was turning up nothing and the police were being strongly pressured to find something quick. And then something finally broke.

During the search of Roxanne's room at home, Lieutenant Franklin found a diary. Written in the daily articles of her diary were incidents of secret meetings between her and Randy, Jennifer's boyfriend. The two of them had been meeting each other for over six months at different quiet places throughout town. The details of her diary left no doubt that a secret affair had been taking place behind Jennifer and Johns back, so Randy's name suddenly darted to the forefront of the investigation.

Randy Bigby was what many would call not the average college kid. He was extremely good-looking, was one of the most popular guys in school, a great athlete in all sports, and real popular with the girls.

His dirty blonde hair, striking blue eyes, and muscular build, attracted all the females to him, but his personality soon chased them away. Not to say that he had a rotten, bastardly personality, but he was like Stephanie, the kind of person who was good-looking and knew it. He knew he had no problems getting the attention of the girls, so he played that to his advantage.

Randy worked part time at the local tanning salon, so the continuous tan he displayed year round helped his good looks even more. Randy and Jennifer had been on and off boyfriend-girlfriend all through middle school and high school and it was well known that her love for him was always and forever, in fact most say that she idolized him. Her devoted girlfriends had continually pleaded with her through the years to forget him and move on to someone who shared the love she had to give, but Jennifer just couldn't. For every time that he cheated on her with another girl she would get mad for a few days, then just take him back. She was hopelessly in love.

By college they seemed to have worked a lot of things out and they were just about inseparable. Randy seemed to mature a little bit and gave Jennifer all of his time and flooded her with love, good times, and gifts. Jennifer was so happy because she felt she had finally gotten the love from Randy she had wanted for so long...or so it seemed!

Before talking to Randy, Lieutenant Franklin approached many of Randy's friends to see if any of them volunteered any information regarding Randy's activities. He didn't reveal to them the facts of the diary, but tried to pry out of them the inner secrets of the group of friends who spent so much time together. None of the girls in the group knew anything of the affair either, or so it seemed. Lieutenant Franklin asked Randy to visit him in the office the next day that he wanted to go over a few details with him.

Randy arrived at the police station at about ten in the morning and the two of them sat down in one of the interview rooms. It was the typical cold dimly lit room that you see in all the police shows, with a table and four chairs in the center of the room, nothing on the walls, except for one wall which had the standard glass mirrored wall, obviously a two-way glass. They greeted each other, sipped on morning coffee, and casually threw around some idle chit-chat to break the ice.

The lieutenant broke away from the casual chatter.

"Tell me Randy. Have you been perfectly honest about everything you have said to me during these two murder investigations? What I mean is have you been thorough in all the details of your relationship with these two girls?"

"Well sure, "answered Randy in a strong yet questionable tone, "I've told you everything I can think of."

"Are you absolutely sure? Now is the time to think hard and not hide any details or secrets from me."

Randy began a jittery motion with his hands sweeping them back and forth across the tabletop as if sweeping away a layer of stubborn dust.

"Yeah I'm sure, "he answered in a low voice as he continually stared down at the tabletop. "Why do you keep asking me that? You know how close Jenn and I were to each other and Roxy was her best friend and mine too. We loved each other like family."

The lieutenant slowly pushed his chair back from the table and began to walk ever so casually around the outside of the room. His hands clasped behind his back and his eyes just staring at the floor as he walked. He silently paraded around each wall just slowly putting one foot in front of another and glaring at the floor. Randy's tabletop dusting stopped as he leaned back in his chair and watched his roommate slowly gliding around the room.

"Now would not be the time to withhold any information from me," the lieutenant's voice broke the silence within the room.

"I'm telling you I've told you everything there is to tell. What more do you want from me?"

"What I want from you is what I have been asking for the past eight weeks, every detail of your life with these two girls; everything that happened between you and them. You are not telling me everything there is to know. It would be much better to hear the truth from you right now."

Randy was silent this time and did not immediately come back with a sharp answer as he had every other time. He stared back down at the table for a minute, then back to the lieutenant who was still slowly walking around and around the walls of the room.

"I will take silence as an admission of no new information."

Again silence from Randy.

"Okay, then we'll do this my way. Tell me about you and Roxanne. Tell me about your secret meetings together behind Jennifer's back. Tell me about the secret love affair you have been having with Jennifer's best friend. Tell me how you have been making love to both of these girls for six months and now they are both dead? I want the truth and I want it now Randy."

Randy leaned back toward the table as he again began to sweep his hands back and forth across the tabletop. Tears slowly began to descend from his watery eyes as the silence was broken by his sobbing.

"How did you ever find out about Roxy and I, no one knew about that but her and I. How could you possibly know about us?"

"How I find out things is not important Randy, what's important is that you tell me the truth and not hold anything back from me."

The lieutenant walked over to the table opposite Randy, pushed the chair seat between his legs and sat down facing Randy with his hands on the chair back. He reached in his pocket and pulled out pictures of the two dead girls and placed them on the table in front of Randy.

"Randy, did you kill these two girls?"

"No," shouted Randy in a sobbing boyish voice, "no I didn't kill them. I loved them both, I wouldn't think of hurting either one of them."

The lieutenant stared directly into his eyes without saying a word.

"Stop staring at me like that. I didn't hurt either one of them, I loved them both," Randy yelled as he pounded his fist on the table with one hand and turned the two pictures over face down.

"Stop it Randy, stop it now," the lieutenant yelled back as he jumped up and threw his chair to the floor. "Stop your pitiful crying and tell me the truth. You loved both of these girls and you didn't really mean to fall in love with both of them. You felt guilty about making love to Roxanne behind Jennifer's back and Roxanne was threatening to tell on you. You tried to tell Jennifer the truth but she became violent with you so you put your hand over her mouth and killed her. Roxanne couldn't believe what you had done to her best friend and threatened to tell the police, so you killed her too to shut her up. She was the only one who could tell the truth about you and her so..."

"Shut up, shut up," Randy yelled, "that's not true. I didn't do it, I didn't do it!"

His voice trailed off to a merciful cry. He buried his head in his arms on top of the table and began to cry like a baby.

"Randy now is the time to get this over with. Get the guilt that has been bottled up inside of you out in the open. Just tell me the truth and it will all be over with. No more guilt, no more hidden secrets, no more running from the truth."

Randy just continued to cry, not even lifting his head off of the table.

"Well I'm considering holding you for these crimes until I get to the truth…so just think about that for a while." The lieutenant reached over and flipped the pictures back face up on the table, walked to the door, opened it, and walked out closing it behind him. He turned the corner and approached his captain and two other detectives that had been working the case with him.

"Let's let him think about things for a while," he said as he headed down the hallway for a cup of coffee.

"Doesn't sound like he's changing his story?" yelled one of the detectives as he too started to leave the observation window.

"I know…I know," the lieutenant said in a low disgusted voice.

They watched as Randy pulled the two pictures in front of himself on the table, and wiped the tears from his cheeks. He rested his head down on top of the two pictures and continued to sob.

6

Nothing more happened during Randy's interrogation and he was released to go home. Once his parents found out about the incident they contacted their lawyer and the investigating team was informed not to make contact with Randy again without his lawyer and parents present.

It didn't take long for rumors to spread throughout the neighborhood that Randy had become a prime suspect in the murders so his friends rallied around him in support as each voiced their total belief in how ridiculous the accusations were. Many of the girls were surprised beyond belief that they had known nothing of the affair between Randy and Roxanne and more surprised that Jennifer had known nothing about it. Roxanne and Jenn were super tight and told each other everything, or at least she thought, and beyond that, they couldn't believe that Roxanne would do such a thing behind Jennifer's back. Of course none of this suppressed any of their sad feelings over what had happened to their two best friends. Many of the girls spent a lot more time together, especially at each other's house, talking of the tragedy and feeling totally terrified knowing the killer was still on the loose.

Throughout the remainder of the summer the investigation continued but no real leads surfaced to help catch the criminal. Since no one else knew of the telltale clues left at the crime scene, namely the messages, talk of a serial killer never surfaced at all. Jennifer's parents and Roxanne's parents spent a lot of time together visiting and consoling. Jennifer's parents were attending family counseling twice a week since the entire ordeal had been so tough on their family. Jack, her brother, never really came out of his shell after her death and they were really concerned for his well being. Jennifer was a huge part of his life and losing someone you look up to so much is devastating to say the least, especially for a fourteen-year-old.

Towards the end of summer Fran's parents threw another party, although it was called more of a gathering than a party, and invited all the kids in the group as well as all their parents; kind of a gathering of everyone involved in the tragedy. Everyone showed up except for Randy and his parents who had become quite secluded since the accusations against their son had surfaced. Fran's dad called over to Randy's house about an hour after everyone else arrived and pleaded with them to come to the gathering, saying how much good it would do everyone to have them all together, so they agreed and arrived about an hour later.

Much of the talk that afternoon was not about what had taken place, but about Jennifer and

Roxanne and how much they had meant in everyone's lives. It wasn't an afternoon of tears, although many people present bravely fought back to keep the tears away. There was a lot of hugging, a lot of talk of the old days, and a lot of talk about the future. College classes would be starting up in another two weeks and everyone in the crowd was eager for summer to be over and a new school year to start. It was kind of a closure to the summer and the tragedies that had engulfed all of them.

Lieutenant Franklin heard about the party and paid a courtesy call to visit with everyone in a more casual atmosphere. He was accompanied by his wife who was accustomed to the demands and stress associated with his job, so she was excellent at presenting her strong yet calming personality to the situation. She usually huddled with the wives and daughters while he talked with the husbands and guys. They usually tried to keep the conversation away from the cases and what was happening although obviously that didn't always happen.

Everyone involved was at this gathering with the exception of Brad, as before. The lieutenant made a point to ask Becky where he was and she reiterated that again he had to work. He nodded in acceptance of her answer but thought it strange that he would miss both affairs thrown by Fran and Becky's parents during the summer. He knew that Brad was very close to her and her family and spent so much time with Becky that missing a chance to see her just seemed suspicious.

As the beginning of a new week started, the investigation team gathered at police headquarters to try and piece together any new leads or evidence that had materialized over the past few weeks.

"Let's see what we have here," said Lt. Franklin as he wheeled over the bulletin board that had all the case facts on it. "We have two girls that were close friends and hung out with the same crowd. We have both murders with the same characteristics and the same clues. We are dealing with a definite male murderer. None of the guys in the crowd have any past records and all have alibi's for their whereabouts on those two nights."

"Except Brad Townsend who said he was home alone," interrupted one of the investigators.

"Yes Brad Townsend. We have questioned him a couple of times but I want to question him again, and maybe apply a little pressure to see how he handles it. We don't know too much about him except that he moved here from Pittsburgh a little over a year ago and opened this photography business. He has a clean record except for a couple traffic violations and has been clean down here. He smokes, or at least says he does occasionally and is trying to quit, and he lives alone over top of his studio."

He was interrupted again by Inspector Burton. "It just seems suspicious with this 24-year-old guy moving into town and taking up with an 18, 19-year-old crowd of kids who pretty much stay to themselves. How did he meet them anyway?"

"I don't know how that all took place, we'll have to ask him," answered the lieutenant as he sipped on his cup of coffee. "I just know he is very, very close to the fifteen-year-old Becky and that just doesn't sit right with me. I mean the whole Thomas family is close to him and approves of him but it just seems like a little more than photography to me. I think they're both hiding something and I intend to find out what that is. Now, we've just about eliminated all the kids and all the parents, so what else do we have."

Inspector Wiley jumped in. "Well we canvassed the neighborhood for two blocks surrounding the Connelly house and the houses closest to where Roxanne's car was found. No success there, we came up empty. We interviewed Jennifer's fellow workers at the bank and none of them really knew too much about her except what happened in the bank. I think that's because most of them are older, in their late twenties and thirties, so they don't really have a lot in common with her outside of work. Roxanne of course didn't work, she attended college and speaking with her professors and classmates led us nowhere."

Lt. Franklin continued to sip his coffee and study the bulletin board. "Okay, so we have exhausted the family, the friends, the co-workers, the school friends, and come up empty-handed. If this guy is murdering girls he knows, then there has to be a link somewhere, unless the link is just pretty girls in this neighborhood and I don't believe that for a minute. These guys always have some link, some reason; something tying everything together and I want to find out what that is."

"How about digging a little deeper into their pasts," said Inspector Burton. "They all graduated together from high school not too long ago, so let's dig into their high school days."

"Sounds good to me," said the lieutenant. "Let's find out what these two girls have in common and let's find it before this guy rapes and murders number three. If that happens, this community and the media will be down our throats and fast...not to mention the Chief."

7

It was a beautiful September fall day and college classes were only about a week from starting so everyone was enjoying their last full week of freedom before the drudgery of daily college life, and hitting the books completely took over their life.

Becky was the only one back in school already since she was fifteen, almost sixteen, and attending Forest Hill High School as a junior, her next to last year. Brad and Becky had spent a lot of the summer together both at his studio and around the town, taking pictures of her for her portfolio that he was compiling. Sometimes he would just follow her around taking candid shots, which really embarrassed her and she'd plead with him to stop, but he would just laugh and keep snapping pictures of her as he called her his young beautiful vivacious star.

"Cut it out Brad," she'd yell, "you're making me mad. Stop taking pictures of me out in public, it's embarrassing."

"Okay, but just until this afternoon. You're much more beautiful in the evening hours. That's when your real beauty comes out."

Many a day during the summer the two of them would be at the beach swimming, sunbathing, and of course taking pictures. Brad had always treated Becky with the utmost respect and never really let on that he had feelings for her. Becky was obviously taken with him because of his good looks, great personality, and most of all the way he treated her; not like a fifteen-year-old but like a friend and companion regardless of age. Most of her friends and family looked at the close relationship as purely professional and friendly in nature, romantic ideas never entered into their minds.

September 19th was Becky's sixteenth birthday and many plans had been made by both her family and friends to celebrate her sweet sixteen. Brad was certainly a part of both celebrations and she was flooded with gifts, hugs, and constant jokes about being 'sweet sixteen and never kissed'.

That day was filled with excitement but Brad wanted to celebrate with Becky alone, just her and him at the studio, which is where they spent most of their time. He asked her to meet him the next day after school, saying he had a surprise of his own for her.

Becky arrived at the studio to find Brad sitting at his processing table cutting negatives. She was excited about meeting him since the two of them had become such close friends throughout the summer, to the point of almost seeing each other daily.

"Hey Brad," she said as she walked in the door shutting it behind her.

"Hey Beck, come on in, I'll be through here in a moment."

"Processing more of my pictures?" she asked with a snide grin on her face.

"No beautiful, not pictures of you! These are pictures I took last week down at the beach of sunsets and sunrises. I do have a life besides you ya' know."

"Oh really," Becky remarked as she pulled up a stool across from him and flipped her long blonde hair off her face and behind her. "I thought I was your favorite subject of choice...guess I was wrong."

"Now, now...you know you're my one and only. I love to take shots of beautiful things, like sunsets, sunrises, nature, and you; all things of natural beauty."

His hand reached out and grabbed her hand as their fingers entangled together and their eyes met, words were not necessary to fulfill the moment. Through all of their time together they had never looked at each other in this way before. Brad had made sure he would do nothing to let her know how he had become infatuated with her, but now the time had come. He didn't need to say anything; he just wanted to let his eyes do the talking at this point.

Becky's heart was pounding as she managed to say, "You said you had a surprise for me today?"

"Yes," he said as he snapped out of his stare and smiled with delight. He gently let go of her hand as his fingers glided out of her grasp. He reached under the table and pulled out a large album that had her name written across the front in Old English Script.

"I've finished your portfolio."

Her eyes widened as she gazed at the beautiful album cover and slid it towards herself. It was white with blue lettering, her two favorite colors together.

"Oh Brad, it's beautiful."

"No Becky, the beauty is inside...the beauty is all you. Happy Birthday."

He leaned over to kiss her on the cheek, but she quickly turned and their lips met ever so softly as they parted four or five times barely making it a kiss. Her hand moved to the back of his head as she pulled him closer and pressed her lips against his. After savoring the passion in her lips Brad finally slowly pulled away.

"Beck...are you sure you want this to happen? I don't want anything to ruin the closeness we have together."

Becky slowly sat back down on her stool, brushed her hair from her face, and flashed her big blue eyes back at Brad. Her gorgeous smile lit up her perfect face which looked more the part of an eighteen-year-old rather than a sixteen-year-old, which was the reason she never looked out of place with her sister Fran's friends or with Brad when they were together.

She moved her hand over her heart as she answered, "Brad, I've never wanted anything more in my whole life. I've had these feelings for you all summer but I wasn't sure how you really felt about me. If you really have feelings for me, then I couldn't be happier...I'm yours if you want me."

Brad moved off of his stool and walked around the table towards her, never taking his eyes off of hers. She stood up as he approached and their outstretched arms embraced each other. He pulled her close in to his body running his hands up and down her back.

"I've wanted to do this all summer. I've wanted to hold you, and hug you, and embrace you since I first laid eyes on you. Kissing you is all I think about."

They pulled apart and looked at each other again as Becky reiterated her feelings looking into his eyes, "I've always had feelings for you but have always been afraid that you felt I was just Fran's little sister who liked to have her picture taken. I can't believe we wasted the whole summer without being together."

"But we were together all summer Beck, we were just getting to know each other and be sure of our feelings...even though we weren't sure how the other one felt."

He pressed his forefinger to her lips saying, "Let's not dwell on what could have happened this summer, let's just enjoy the moment and how we feel about each other. Now can I please kiss you again?"

She smiled and wrapped her hands around the back of his neck as she pulled him close. "Any time you want."

Their heads came together again as his lips slowly touched hers. He gently pulled back and ran his tongue over the surface of her lips as he again pressed his lips to hers. This time their kiss was strong and long as her tongue went into his mouth playing tag with his tongue. The excitement was evident as their combined breathing became louder and louder, their bodies rubbing up and down against each other.

Brad slowly pulled back from her, catching his breath.

"Let's not get too carried away right now. You have to be home soon," he said as he glanced back over his shoulder looking at the clock.

"Okay," she said, "you know what's best. I just want to be with you, near you."

"I know, but let's be smart and control our feelings and emotions. The last thing we want to do now is jeopardize things by you being late on a school night. Let's enjoy what we have discovered and take it home with us. Okay?"

"Whatever you say Brad," Becky said as she kissed his cheek and began to gather her books together. She had often stopped by his studio on the way home from school, but knew she had to be home by five for dinner. Her parents were real lenient with her as far as her schedule right after school, but their rule had always been that they all eat dinner together as a family, then it's homework after dinner before television or telephone time. Her feelings for Brad certainly would be no excuse for being late for dinner.

They decided to keep their relationship quiet for a while. Becky just didn't feel like taking the fifth degree from her sister for dating a twenty-four-year-old guy, especially since he was older than Fran and older than anyone in their entire crowd. So it was their secret for a while.

She continued to meet Brad after school every day and couldn't wait until the weekend arrived so they could really spend some time together.

8

The weekend finally arrived and Becky couldn't wait to get down to Brad's studio. She called him as soon as the family finished breakfast and agreed to visit with him around noon. She knew it would take her at least two hours to get ready, put her makeup on, and dress for this occasion, but a whole day with Brad meant she wanted to look her best and wanted everything perfect for their first whole day together since her birthday surprise.

Brad's studio was only a ten minute walk from her house and she spent that time just daydreaming about the two of them together. She had spent so many nights just dreaming about Brad and her together and wondering how he felt about her, but now she knew it was real and knew that Brad had feelings for her too and her heart pounded just thinking about it.

She got to the studio, peeked into the window, and saw him working at the cutting table.

"Too busy for some company?" she asked as she opened the door and walked in.

"Yeah sure...that'll be the day I'm too busy for you," he answered as he pushed the film aside and looked up at her. "Wow, you outdid yourself today...you look fantastic. Not that you don't always look fantastic, but whew, you do look mighty fine."

"Well thank you sir, I try to please my favorite people."

"I have to develop a few negatives in the dark room...care to join me?"

"Just lead the way," Becky answered as she followed through the doorway and closed the door behind her.

Brad clicked on the red light in the room as he laid the negatives on the table. He turned to Becky and held out his hands towards her. She placed her hands into his and moved next to him as close as she could get. Tightly they pressed against each other as their lips were locked in a passionate embrace. They separated as they looked into each other's eyes, letting their eyes again do the talking.

Becky took Brads hand and moved it to her heart.

"Feel how strongly my heart is racing just being near you."

Brad's hand lay motionless on her breast as the pounding of her heart echoed throughout her whole body. She reached up again and this time moved his hand down to engulf her whole breast.

"Please love me," she said as her eyes filled with the passion of their closeness. She shivered with excitement as his hand lay motionless on her breast. Becky was a virgin but had been quite intimate over the past two years with numerous boys. She knew what playfulness was all about and knew just how far to go to tease the guys and drive them crazy. But she also knew when to stop, when the playfulness was going too far. This drove the guys crazy because besides looking more like she is eighteen than sixteen, her body had been very well developed ever since she was about thirteen-years-old.

Brad cupped his hand around and over her breast caressing the outline of her perfect bosom. His eyes never left hers as no words were spoken, only the movement of his hand. He moved his other hand from behind her back to her other breast. His hands moved in tandem as he massaged her blouse as their breathing began to break the silence. He moved the fingers of both hands to the center of her blouse as he began to slowly unbutton each of the buttons. One by one his fingers moved to each button until he was finished and her blouse was falling open. He moved each side of the blouse off of her shoulder and finally off of her completely. Her firm round breasts protruded out of the top of her white lace trimmed bra as if trying to escape their restricted space. Her size 35 breasts were firm and round and raced with excitement as they rapidly moved up and down with her excitement. Brad cupped his hands over her bra and gently moved his fingers to the edges and then inside. His eyes moved from her eyes to her body as he moved his hands up to her shoulders and to her bra straps. As the straps moved off her shoulders she let each one fall and slowly moved each arm up and through each one. Moving his hands to her back he grasped her bra clasp and snapped it open as she reached up and removed the bra from her body. He stepped slightly back from her as his eyes darted taking in every inch of her upper body.

"I thought you were absolutely beautiful before, but now I see that I haven't even begun to see how beautiful you are. Every inch of you is simply gorgeous. I just love looking at you Becky. Thank you."

The excitement of him looking at her engulfed her whole body, but she wanted more of him. She closed her eyes and let her head fall back allowing her long blonde hair to cascade off her shoulders and down her back. Brad bent down to her long bare neck and moved his lips to touch ever so softly. He moved slowly from one side of her neck to the other kissing her and toying with his tongue. Her hands moved to the back of his hair as she edged his head further down her body.

"Wait," Brad said as he grabbed her hands to stop her, "this is not the time or place for us." His breathing was rapid as he clasped his fingers into hers. "Let's wait and enjoy this moment when it's just right, when it's perfect, okay?"

Her eyes stared directly into his as he rose up and moved his hands to each side of her face, cupping her cheeks in each hand.

"Brad I've never wanted anything more. I want to make love to you."

"I know Beck, I want you more than I've wanted anything before, but I don't want to make love to you in a darkroom under a red light. I want to see your natural beauty and hold and caress you in a romantic place, not here. Let's wait okay?"

"Okay," Becky answered as she took a deep breath.

Brad again moved his hands and his eyes down to her bare chest as he just continued to take in all of her.

"You are so very beautiful, I love every inch of you that I've seen so far."

He bent down to pick up her bra and blouse and moved behind her helping her put each one on. Once she had her blouse buttoned and tucked in, he wrapped his arms around her body to the front of her waist and clasping his hands pulled her back against his chest in a tight hug.

"I can feel your excitement," she said as her bottom pressed back against the front of his pants. He moved quickly and spun her around so they were face to face. He pulled her close and gave her a huge bear hug letting out a giant sigh of relief.

"Oh Becky, Becky, Becky...how am I ever going to leave you today?"

"I'm yours all day long so do whatever you want with me," Becky said as she smiled and winked at his handsome face.

The day was young so they decided to get Brad's dog and take him over to the park, where they had first met, and run around playing for a while. The dog loved the outdoors and they played with him continually throwing a ball, a stick, a Frisbee, and anything else they could find. The three of them ran up and down the park for what seemed like hours until they finally collapsed on the green grass. As they lay on the ground in each other's arms their lips again met in a passionate embrace until Sampson, Brad's dog, began licking both of their faces.

"Okay Sampson, we'll pay more attention to you now," laughed Brad as he pushed the dogs head away from theirs. He gently gave her another quick kiss on the lips as he pulled her up and suggested they take Sampson home and then go get something to eat.

"Let's go to Bay Café for lunch," he suggested as they began to walk towards home, "I want to go someplace real nice where we can talk, okay?"

"Wow, a nice lunch in a quiet place, sounds serious to me."

They walked home hand in hand with Sampson leading the way as she agreed to the suggested place. Her mind wandered as she wondered what he wanted to talk about but she cast her thoughts aside as they walked and laughed along the way.

Brad chose a secluded table by the window facing the water, lit only by candlelight and the faint overhead lights of the restaurant. They each ordered a glass of water with a lemon twist, a favorite likeness of both of them. After their sandwiches were ordered, Brad pulled Becky close to the table as he gazed in her bright blue eyes across from him.

"Beck, I wanted to talk to you about our relationship that is about to blossom. I wanted to get your feelings on something before we get too far along."

"Okay," she answered, "is there something wrong? You're scaring me."

"No, no....nothing wrong," Brad answered back. "I just want to get us both prepared. We will be facing our friends and families soon, together as a couple, and I'm just not sure how everyone will take the news of us together intimately. I mean it makes no difference to you or me, but you are sixteen, and I am twenty-four, and many people may not like that."

"But I don't care what they think. Do you? Does it matter what other people think or does it matter how we feel about each other?" snapped Becky, defending her feelings.

"I know you don't care, and neither do I, I love you no matter what. But you have to think about everyone around us. I mean your parents will flip out because they have trusted us to be together so much because of my profession and the thought of you as a model. If they thought I was using photography to get close to their daughter, they would flip out and the last thing we want is for your parents to break our relationship apart, I mean at sixteen they still are in control of your life and can really make life miserable for both of us."

"So what are you saying?" asked Becky as a tear rolled down her cheek.

Brad reached up to capture the trailing tear from her cheek.

"No Beck, now don't get upset. I'm not suggesting that we break up or stop seeing each other. All I'm suggesting is that we keep our feelings for each other quiet for a while. Let's not spring it on everyone all at once. Let's just keep things the way they are on the outside, while we get to know each other on the inside."

Becky reached up with a napkin and wiped her eyes. Her head was bowed down toward the table as her long blonde hair tickled the edges of the tabletop. Brad reached over and lifted her chin towards him while kissing his fingers and planting it on her lips.

"What do ya say?" he asked.

"I guess you're right," she whispered in a low faint sad tone. "I just love you so much I want to tell the world. But I don't want to do anything that may jeopardize us being together so I guess we'll keep it between us for a while."

"Okay now, that means we have to act the way we used to act when we're out around our friends, especially when your sister Fran is around. We have to be good friends and business partners like we have in the past. No holding hands or spur of the moment kisses. Agreed?"

"Well it's not going to be easy," she said in a pouting voice. "But if you can take it, I guess I can too. Does that mean I have to wait forever for our special moment together that we talked about today?"

"Yes Beck we really have to wait a little while for that. Believe me, it's gonna be real tough for me being with you all the time, especially when we're alone together, not to be able to go all the way with you, but you have to remember that you just turned sixteen and if anyone thought we were having sex I could be put in jail for the rest of my life for having sex with a minor. I'm not saying that is keeping me from doing it, or that we won't do it until you're older; I'm just saying we have to be real careful so as not to ruin it for both of us. Just bear with me for a while, it'll be okay. I promise."

"Okay, but it's not going to be easy, especially after today," she said as her foot rubbed against the inside of his leg.

9

As the weeks passed, Becky and Brad played their two separate roles, one as outside friends and the other as inside lovers. They did an especially good job because no one suspected anything at all was going on between them, so their plan was working perfectly. They continued to pal around with the crowd and play their friendship game, but when it came to Brad's studio and photography time, things were a lot different.

Early in October Brad told Becky he was going to be busy developing all the pictures he'd taken of the whole crowd down at the park the weekend before. She said she'd stop by, but he insisted he needed the time alone to get things done. When she was there all of his attention went towards her, not the photography equipment. She reluctantly agreed.

As the night went on, Becky was home but became increasingly sad and lonely without him since they had spent just about every free moment together, even though no one really knew. Her friends in the crowd, and even her sister, commented to her that she wasn't around much anymore, but Becky just used her high school studies as her excuse and everyone understood that.

But on this night she was completely restless without him and decided to go out and pull a surprise visit on him at the studio. Her dad was out of town on business so she told her mom and sister she was going to the library to do some research on a school project and that she'd be home in about two hours. Fran offered to drive her but Becky insisted she needed some time to herself and the walk would do her good. It still stayed light until almost eight at night, so they didn't think twice about her safety from home to there and back.

She gathered her things together and walked at a fast pace to Brad's studio, excited about seeing and surprising him. She could just taste his lips on hers as she unknowingly moistened them with her tongue at the thought of seeing him.

To her surprise as she arrived at the studio everything was dark. She tried both the front and back door but both were locked tight as she looked in but couldn't see any lights in the studio or in his upstairs apartment. Everything was dark and silent.

She was puzzled by everything but more so worried that maybe something had happened. Why would Brad have said he was going to be here when in fact he wasn't? Something had to be wrong. Well, maybe something just came up unexpectedly. No worry!

She turned and slowly walked home trying to use up some time, but wanting to get there before dusk. She arrived home, told her mom she didn't feel well, and went to her room where she tried to call him on his cell phone but there wasn't an answer. Where could he be? She decided to leave him a message to call her as soon as he got in. She lay down on her bed, clicked her radio on softly, and slowly drifted off to sleep, to the sound of a jet flying overhead and a faint siren heard in the distance.

Becky awoke to the buzz of her alarm going off, but was startled as she rolled over to see her mother shutting it off.

"Mom, you scared me...what are you doing up here this early? I can't believe I fell asleep and slept all night in my clothes."

Her mom sat down on the edge of the bed.

Becky could see a tear in her eye and a trembling motion in her hands. "Mom, what's wrong, you're scaring me," Becky asked as she sat up in bed and grabbed her mother's shaking hands.

"Becky dear, I don't know how to tell you this," her voice quivered as the words slowly and painfully came out, "but last night something terrible happened."

Becky's heart skipped a beat as panic took control of her eyes as she immediately thought of Brad and not being able to find him the night before.

"No Mom, no Mom, no Mom...don't tell me!" she yelled as her hands went up to cover her face and ears. "Please Mom, don't tell me something's happened to him, please Mom, please!"

"Happened to who dear, who are you talking about Becky?" her mom asked as she moved Becky's hands from her face and wiped her eyes.

Serial

G. Lusby

"Brad, something's happened to Brad, I know it," Becky sobbed.

"No dear, what makes you think something's happened to your friend Brad; why would you suddenly think that Becky?"

Becky got a surprised look on her face as joy replaced the grief that had engulfed her.

"Because on the way to the library last night I stopped by his studio and he wasn't there. He had told me he'd be there all night working on a bunch of pictures he took of all of us at the park last weekend. I left him a message but he never returned my call all night long. But if it's not Brad, then what happened, what's the bad news Mom? It's not Dad is it?"

Becky's mom again took hold of her hand as her soft voice rang out the words of terror.

"No it's not your father dear, but last night we got word that Margy was found murdered behind the store where she works."

"Oh my God," screamed Becky, "not Margy too! Oh my God. What happened?"

"Her boyfriend Peter called late last night and wanted to talk to you, but I told him you were asleep and we didn't want to disturb you because you went to bed not feeling well. All he told us was that the police got a call from the owner of the store that when he went back last night to close up, the store was locked but the light was on in the back room, so he went back to turn it off and found Becky lying in the floor dead. That's all we know dear."

"God Mom, I wonder if it was just like Jenn and Roxanne. Mom I'm scared."

"I know dear, we all are. We told your sister first thing this morning and she left to drive over to Peter's house to talk to him about what happened."

"So Fran already knows?" asked Becky.

"Yes. She's obviously not going to classes today and we don't think you should go to school either. I called your father on his cell and he went right from the airport over to see Mr. and Mrs. McNichol to see if there is anything we can do to help."

"How was Peter when he called?"

Her mother just shook her head as tears ran down her cheeks. "He was a real basket case to say the least. You know Margy and him have known each other since elementary school."

"I know…they've been boyfriend and girlfriend since the third grade I think. He has to be devastated. Oh Mom I'm so scared. What if they were all murdered by the same person; maybe even someone who knows all of us."

"I know dear. Your father and I are hoping that the police will call some kind of meeting with all of us to discuss what's been going on. We need to know all the details so we can make the right decisions to protect ourselves."

Becky buried her face back in her pillow as she sobbed over what was happening to her friends. Her mom pulled the sheets back up over her and rubbed her back.

"I'm going downstairs dear in case someone else calls. You get some rest and try not to think about it too much. We'll get to the bottom of this, I promise."

Becky continued to lie in bed quietly sobbing as she thought of yet another friend who had been lost. It wasn't too long after her mother left the room that she heard the phone ring, just one ring and it stopped. Becky got up out of bed and slipped on her jeans and a tee-shirt and headed downstairs to see who had called.

Her mom was just hanging up the phone on the kitchen wall when Becky entered.

"Who was that Mom?"

"Becky, why are you up dear, you should get some rest," her mom answered as she came over to hug her.

"Who was on the phone Mom?"

"It was your father. He's on his way home from the McNichol's house and wanted to let me know."

"Did he say anything else?" Becky asked.

"No, just that he was on his way home and we would talk once he got here. He asked me if you and Fran were here and I told him your sister was over Peter's house. He's going to stop by there on the way home and tell Fran to come home so we can all talk. Do you want some breakfast sweetheart?"

"No mom, I can't eat. I'm going up to take a shower before Dad and Fran get back."

"Okay dear."

Once her dad and sister got home, they all huddled together in the living room to talk over the incident. Bob and Julie Thomas were very protective of their two daughters and certainly were very concerned over the three murders of their close friends.

"I'm not going to ground you girls," said their dad, "because we all have our lives to live and we're not going to let some lunatic murderer disrupt our daily lives, but, what I do want is for both of you to be very, very careful. Do not, and I repeat, do not, travel around alone. You are both expected to always have someone else with you at all times. Is that understood?"

Both of the girls nodded as they both sat together in one single plush chair huddled close together.

"Now it is my understanding that the police are asking all of the parents of your friends to gather tonight down at police headquarters to discuss the situation. So your mother and I will be going down there tonight at seven o'clock. While we are gone, and every time you girls are alone in the house, I want all doors locked securely. Never feel you are protected just because you are in your safe warm surroundings. Always lock the doors, always lock your car doors, and always carry your cell phones wherever you go. Any questions?"

"No Dad," answered Fran.

It was a short drive to the police station as Bob and Julie arrived a few minutes before seven and parked in the visitors' lot next to the main building. The lot was fairly full so they assumed most of the parents had already arrived.

Once inside, they were directed to the small meeting room which was crowded with people seated in folding chairs. As they sat down they were greeted by many of their close friends and could see as they looked around that everyone was present including the parents of the three murdered girls.

It was a small cold looking room with gray bare walls except for an occasional wanted poster scattered here and there. The only other furniture in the room was an empty blackboard positioned in the front of the room.

At precisely seven o'clock Lieutenant Franklin and three other men, two dressed in suits and one in a police uniform entered the room.

"Ladies and gentlemen, if I could have your attention please," snapped Lieutenant Franklin as they moved to the front of the room. "First we would like to thank you for taking the time from your busy schedules to come down here tonight, we appreciate that. As most of you know, I am Lieutenant Will Franklin, to my right are Inspectors Tom Willey and George Burton, and to my left is our Chief of Police Chester Dawson. On behalf of all of us we welcome you on this solemn and very sad night. We are here to not only inform you of the information we have gathered so far in these murder investigations, but to advise you on what precautions you and your family should take in the future. Afterwards we will open the floor to any questions you may have which we will be happy to answer if we can. Please understand that there may be certain kinds of information that we will not divulge at this time since all three murders are still being investigated. I will first turn the floor over to Inspector Burton who will review the details we have so far."

Inspector Burton stepped forward as the other three men moved to the side.

"Good evening. First I would like to express my sincere sympathies to the three families that are here tonight as grieving parents. Mr. and Mrs. Connelly, Mr. and Mrs. Willowby, and Mr. and Mrs. McNichol, thank you so much for coming under the current circumstances. The loss of these three girls has devastated not only these families, not only their close friends, and not only this police force, but the entire community as a whole. We want to assure you that we are doing everything within our power to commit as many officers and investigators on this case as we possibly can to capture this person who is terrorizing our neighborhood. Lieutenant Franklin has been the lead investigator on this case since the first murder took place and will continue to command this force through the entire investigation and to the final capture. Tonight our plans are to review the details of the three murders with you, making you aware of the information we have gathered so far, and hopefully, some of this information may lead you to remember some small detail that has not surfaced yet. This is a local crime within our community that seems to have targeted just this small group of girls that have grown up together through school and now college. There have been no reported cases within the state of any murders with these same characteristics. The details we have gathered unmistakably prove to us that these crimes have been committed by one person."

The silence in the room is interrupted by the muttering of voices as the information hits home with each set of parents.

"Please," asked the inspector, "if I could have your attention again. I know a lot of the information you will receive tonight is new to many of you, but please let us present everything to you before you jump to any assumptions. The murder of these three girls has been linked to one person simply by the evidence we have found that is repetitive in each case. We have not found any information that specifically zeros in on one person such as fingerprints or DNA, but we are simply saying that tell-tale clues in each instant leads us to believe that there is one single killer out there targeting this group of girls. And, I am sorry to say, as you will see by the details, it seems to be someone that is familiar to the girls, someone whom they know!"

Again the room becomes alive with the buzzing of voices and gasps as they realize what the inspector has told them.

"I would now like to turn the meeting over to Inspector Tom Willey who will go over the details we have gathered so far."

Inspector Burton moves to the side as the introduced inspector moves to the front of the room beside the blackboard.

"At this time I would like to present to you the information we have gathered so far in these three cases. But first, let me address the parents of Jennifer, Roxanne, and Margy. The details I am about to review may be very upsetting to each of you. If you feel you may not want to see these gruesome facts, please feel free to leave the room at this time and we will call you back in when we have finished. We certainly don't want to upset you more than you have been already."

Each of the three sets of parents, who were sitting together, looked at each other shaking their heads.

"No inspector, we have agreed to stay through this in hopes, as you say, of discovering some information that may lead to this killer. Thanks, but continue," said Todd Connelly, speaking for all three families.

"Okay, very well," the inspector continued as he flipped over the blackboard revealing the other side. "Here we have the three victims in this case."

Flipping the blackboard revealed the bulletin board side. On the board were the three pictures of the girls and details listed under them.

"As you can see by the details listed, each girl was murdered in a familiar place. Jennifer, her house;

Roxanne, her car; and Margy at her place of work. Each girl died of affixation via the blocking of their airways. Each girl was partially stripped of her clothing and raped. In all three cases the killer used rubber gloves, leaving no fingerprints, and used a condom leaving no semen. In each case the body of the victim was wiped clean using an alcohol solution to remove any bodily fluids that the killer may have left. Each of the victims knew each other and attended the same schools and hung in the same crowd; which again leads us to believe that this crowd of kids is being targeted for some reason. There is a definite link to these three murders."

The inspector paused to take a drink of water as the crowd of parents again began to chatter as they snuggled together in disbelief.

"Now," he continued, "at this point in time we have no specific suspects. We have conducted interviews with all of the kids in this group that travel together and after last night's murder, we will interview everyone again. The murder last night of Margy McNichol at her place of work had all the same symptoms of the other murders, nothing different. We came out of this murder with no clues as we did in the other crimes, so we have to rely on the past history of these girls to try and link together the murders. Please do not get upset if we interrogate your children again and again; we are just trying to help them remember any minute detail that may give us the clue that ties everything together. At this point in the investigation, after three successive murders, everyone is a suspect, even all of you."

The hush was again interrupted by voices.

"Please, please bear with us. Our sole objective is to find this person and get them locked behind bars before the next incident occurs."

"Inspector," a voice shouted from the crowd, "are we looking at a serial killer here? Do we have a serial killer murdering our children?"

This prompted the gathering to become completely silent, waiting for an answer.

"We are not at this time going to the media with a quote, serial killer scenario. The last thing we want to do is cause a panic in this community. In many cases the killer wants notoriety and loves when they are talked about in the papers and on TV...we don't want that. We don't want to do anything to encourage this person to kill again. At this time I want to bring up Police Chief Dawson who will advise you on what to do next."

The white haired uniformed police chief moved to the center of the room again waiting for complete silence.

"Ladies and Gentlemen...parents...please do not panic. Please do not let these incidents destroy your life as you know it. You need to advise your children, but do not panic them. They are already devastated by what has happened, so reassure them that we are doing everything to catch this person. Instruct them on how to be safe and not to travel alone. Instruct them on locking the doors and staying away from strangers. Instruct them on being cautious and always traveling with friends in a group, not alone. Most of all, everyone just use simple common sense and don't panic. Pay attention to every detail around you, no matter how small it may seem. If you remember something or see something specific, call us and let us know, anytime, no matter what it is. We need your help and the help of your children to bring this guy to justice; to get him out of our neighborhood and behind bars where he belongs. And last, please give us your complete and honest cooperation whenever we visit your family with questions, and remember we are only trying to bring this to an end and make this community a safe place again. Thank you."

Police Chief Dawson stepped aside and moved back in line with his comrades as Lieutenant Franklin moved to the front.

"At this time I'd like to address any questions any of you might have regarding our investigation. Please just raise your hand if you have a question."

A few hands immediately went up in the crowd.

"Yes Mr. Thomas," the lieutenant motioned as he pointed towards Fran's parents.

"Yes Lieutenant...first on behalf of all of us we'd like to thank each of you for taking the time to meet here with us to discuss these tragedies. Our entire neighborhood is just about going berserk thinking about what has happened. What I was wondering is if you have any clues at all that may lead you to the killer?"

"The clues that we have are minimal. We have found a cigarette butt near two of the three killings, but they are from different brands and have revealed no DNA findings; so they may have nothing whatsoever to do with the killer. In each case the victim's mouth, eyes, and hands were taped with duct tape...but again the killer apparently wore gloves because no prints were recovered in either case. Also, the duct tape is the ordinary store bought kind so we couldn't trace it anywhere specific. We have one other clue that is dominate in each case, but at this time we are choosing not to reveal what it is. That's it!"

The lieutenant pointed toward another raised hand.

"Do you have any specific suspects at this time?"

"No...there are a couple of people that we are continually questioning, but that is only because they were extremely close to the victims or because they may tend to know some details so we are trying to help them remember. Other than that, we leave all options open."

He acknowledged another raised hand in the audience.

"Does it seem like there may be more than one person involved in each incident, or do you think they acted alone."

"At this time, looking at each victim and each murder scene, we believe it is one male killer acting alone. It is obviously a man due to the rape evidence and the strength shown in subduing each of the victims. There is no evidence of multiple intruders. In the first murder the intruder entered through a rear door after cutting a hole in the glass with a glass cutter; but in the second and third murders it seems as if the victims knew the intruder. Roxanne stopped her car voluntarily for someone and Margy opened the back door of her workplace for someone she knew and trusted...so that leads us to believe the intruder was a known acquaintance...possibly."

He pointed towards the last raised hand.

"Have you received any correspondence or phone calls from the killer? Usually a serial killer tries to contact the police or media?"

"No sir, nothing has been received at all. If that is all the questions, we'd again like to thank you for your attendance and your complete cooperation. I will be conducting more individual interviews over the next few days and will be talking personally to each one of you. Again, please assure your children that we are doing everything possible to catch this person and also review with them any safety tips you may deem necessary to ensure their safety. Drive safely and goodnight."

Everyone in the audience stood and began to talk amongst themselves. The three victims parents were surrounded by everyone as words of bereavement were passed back and forth. Everyone slowly made their way out of the building and to their cars, talking continually as they left. The entire night was both informative and frightening as they each thought of the killer possibly being a part of their town.

10

Lieutenant Franklin spent the next few days visiting each of the families whose children were close to the victims. He questioned each of them individually, not only questioning where they were when the murders occurred, but if they knew of anyone at school or work or in the community who might have ever had a problem with any of them. In almost every case he was drawing a complete blank. On this particular afternoon he was spending some time at the Thomas home questioning Fran and Becky and their parents. First he questioned them together as a family.

"Mr. Thomas, were all of you home on the night of Margy's murder?"

"Aaaahhhh, no we weren't," he replied, "I was out of town on business and flying home that night; Julie and Fran were at home; and Becky...where were you Becky?"

"I went to the library to do some research work but didn't feel good so I came home and went to bed."

"And didn't you stop by Brad's studio on the way?" asked her mother Julie.

"Yes, on the way down I stopped by the studio to see if Brad was there, but he wasn't, so I left and went to the library, then home."

"Why did you stop by to see Brad Townsend?" asked the lieutenant.

"Just to say hi, I thought he was going to be there developing some pictures he took of all of us down at the park the weekend before. At least that's what he told me...so I stopped by to say hello."

"Do you stop by his studio often?"

"Yes, Brad and I are real good friends and he has spent a lot of time taking pictures of me for my portfolio in case I decide to model one day."

"Well he certainly knows a beautiful subject when he sees one," he remarked as he smiled and looked towards her parents.

"You have two beautiful daughters."

"Thank you lieutenant," said Bob Thomas as he pulled his wife close to him, "we're very proud of both of them."

"I have talked with Brad Townsend quite a few times and know he is twenty-four-years-old. Do you think it is wise for a fifteen-year-old girl to be hanging around the studio of a good-looking young man who has only lived in this community for a year, Mr. Thomas?"

"I'm sixteen," snapped Becky, "sixteen, not fifteen."

Mrs. Thomas jumped immediately into the conversation.

"We have met Brad and had him over here many times. His close relationship with Becky has purely been on a professional nature that is why she spends so much time at his studio. He is a fine young man and we both feel Becky is safe with him as we would with any professional photographer who lives in this community. The time they have spent together in a professional manner has led to a strong friendship between them and we realize that. Besides, most of the time he has lived in this community he has befriended all of the college kids that our daughters hand around with and is well known and well liked by them and all the parents, so for those reasons we trust and respect him."

"Brad's a great guy...you don't suspect him of anything do you?" asked Becky.

"Again," answered Lieutenant Franklin as he threw his hands up in front of himself in defense, "I'm only exploring all the possibilities. No, Brad is no more a suspect than anyone else is. I just don't want this kind of thing to happen to anyone else in this community, so I can't leave any stone unturned. Don't get mad at me ladies; you're ganging up on me!"

They all laughed as he again put his hands up in defense.

"Becky, can I talk to you alone now?" he asked as he pointed towards the dining room where he had once before spoken with each of them alone after Roxanne's murder.

"Sure."

They walked to the dining room and sat down as he again started questioning the relationship she had with Brad.

"Becky it sure seems like you spend a lot of time at Brad's...is there more going on then you've told me?"

"No," answered Becky as she flipped her hair back over her shoulders and stared at the table top,

"Brad and I see a lot of each other because we became really good friends during our picture sessions all summer long. He's just a really good, really close friend, that's all."

"You seemed surprised when he wasn't at his studio the other night when you stopped by, especially since you thought he would be there. Have you talked to him since, to see why he wasn't there?"

"No I haven't talked to him since Thursday night, the day before Margy was found. I don't know where he was. You don't really suspect him do you? Brad is a great guy and a good friend to all of us…he wouldn't hurt a flea, let alone his best friends."

"Slow down Becky," the lieutenant said as he put his arm around her shoulder. "I don't have any suspicions with Brad or any of the other guys in your crowd, but I have to ask questions and I have to talk to everyone, that's my job. You want this killer found don't you?"

"Well sure I do, we all do," Becky answered as she leaned her head against his arm.

"Okay then, let me do my job. And part of that is finding out everything I can about everyone. Sometimes there's a little itty-bitty clue found in something someone says or does that no one ever thinks about, and I have to find all those little itty-bitty clues. Okay sweetie?"

"Okay," she answered in almost a whisper.

"Now, one last question, does Brad smoke?"

"Yeah sometimes, but not too much anymore; he's trying to quit. I can't really remember the last time I saw him smoking…why do you ask?"

"Oh just curious. Is there anything else you can think of as far as Margy and other people she might have known? Anyone you remember her being with or hanging around outside of your crowd of close friends?"

Becky hesitated, and then said, "No, I really didn't see much of Margy the last few weeks. Her and Peter spend a lot of time together and the crowd hasn't been together a whole lot since school started back up."

"From interviewing them before, sounds like Margy and Peter were real, real close?"

Becky laughed as she answered his question, "Close isn't the word. I mean they've been together forever...since third grade. You hardly ever saw one without the other."

"Well, if you think of anything, anything at all, give me a call or tell your parents, okay?"

"Okay," she answered as she smiled and walked back to the living room.

Lieutenant Franklin finished up with the individual interviews then said his goodbyes. It was early in the evening so he thought he would pay a visit to Brad's studio on his way back to the precinct.

As he arrived he found the studio dark and no lights could be seen upstairs. Repeated knocks to the door ended in silence, so he left and returned to his office.

Early the next morning as Becky was dressing for school her cell phone rang and it was Brad.

"Brad, where have you been for two days, I have tried and tried to reach you at home and your cell phone...where are you?

"I'm so sorry Beck, I had some business to take care of out of town and the time just got away from me. I didn't mean to not call you, I was just real busy so I had my cell turned off...I'm sorry Becky."

"Well you really scared me, I thought maybe something happened to you," Becky said in a strong concerned voice. "It just scared me that you were not in the studio when you said you would be and haven't called in two days. For the past three months we've talked every day, so it just wasn't like you to just disappear and not call me or something. What kind of business did you have and where?"

"I was three hours away at Bethany Beach Delaware tending to some photography business. Again I'm sorry Beck, I didn't mean to just disappear on you, it won't happen again, okay babe?"

"Okay, just don't disappear on me again, I just thought you couldn't live without me for two whole days...I guess I was wrong."

"No babe, you have every right to be mad at me, but believe me this business was important, real important for both of us. I can't go into details now, but trust me, okay?"

Becky believed him and didn't press the issue any more. Now she had to tell him the latest news surrounding the community.

"Brad, there are some other people looking for you also, the police. While you were gone Margy was found murdered just like Jenn and Roxanne."

"Oh my God," interrupted Brad in a startled voice, "when did that happen?"

"Thursday night. Her boss found her dead in the back of the store. She had been raped and killed. All the parents in the community met with the police Friday evening and everyone is assuming now that the same person has committed all three murders. We're like scared to death over here."

"Wow," exclaimed Brad, "how is Peter doing?"

"I haven't talked to him, but Fran has. She said he is pretty shaken up and has gone into a kind of silent mode. He just sits in the house and sobs without talking or eating. I don't even know if he'll go to her funeral, it may be too much for him to handle."

"He'll have to go to her funeral. He'll never forgive himself if he doesn't. I'll have to talk to him. I'll head over there as soon as we hang up. God, three of our best friends murdered, Becky you and Fran have got to be real careful because there is definitely a mad man on the loose…you hear me?"

"I know, Dad has already set some ground rules for Fran and me. We can't travel around by ourselves; we have to be with someone else at all times. And that's fine with me, I don't really want to be by myself anymore, it's scary. The police really think it is someone who knows us all. They have been looking for you to talk to…you should give them a call right away."

"I will. I'll give them a call when we hang up, then go by and see Peter, and I'll stop by to see you later today after you get home from school if that's okay with you?"

She agreed and as they hung up Brad heard his doorbell ringing downstairs. As he ran down the steps and approached the studio door he recognized Lieutenant Franklin standing on the other side.

"Lieutenant," he remarked as he unbolted the door and opened it, "I just got off the phone with Becky and heard what happened. Come on in."

"Thanks Brad, we have all been wondering what happened to you the last few days. No one knew where you were; even your close friend Becky."

"I know. It was really stupid of me to just disappear like that. I just spent twenty minutes on the phone trying to explain myself to her. She kind of freaked out that I didn't at least call her for two days. But I explained everything to her and said I was going to stop by the police station to talk with you since she mentioned you had been looking for me."

"Well you apparently have heard what happened, so why don't you also explain to me where you've been if you don't mind?"

"Sure, no problem! As I told Becky, I've been down Bethany Beach Delaware staying with friends. I'll certainly give you their names if you want to confirm my story; but I'd rather not go into the details of my visit if you don't mind."

"Okay Brad, if that's all you want to tell me. I don't really care what your visit was all about, but I definitely need their names so I can confirm with them. I hope you understand that I have to check all bases in these murder investigations."

Brad agreed and gave him the names and address of his friends in Bethany Beach. He decided to keep the details of his visit to himself at this point in time, it was something he didn't want anyone to know about, especially Becky.

"Do you smoke Brad?" the lieutenant asked while glancing around the room.

"No," he answered, "...well not much anymore, I've been trying to stop but haven't been real successful yet. I've been quitting for some time now and rarely smoke except when I get really nervous and need them to pacify me; in fact I could use one now. I don't know what it is but cops and detectives and judges just freak me out. I've always been that way, real nervous around the law. No offense, I don't mind talking to you lieutenant, I just get nervous dealing with authority."

They finished their short conversation and as the lieutenant walked to the door to leave he had a piece of advice for Brad.

"Let me just say one thing Brad and I'll leave it at that. You're fairly new to this area and this is a very close knit community. It would not be wise to hide secrets from too many people and especially if there is anything going on between you and Becky Thomas. I've talked to her and her family and they all think very highly of you, to the point of justifying your relationship with their daughter. In my eyes you are twenty-four and she is sixteen...I would hope you know what you are doing. Understood?"

"Loud and clear Lieutenant," Brad answered as he opened the door for him to leave.

Later that day Lieutenant Franklin contacted Brad's friends in Delaware and they confirmed that he was in fact there for the better part of two days. He was very suspicious of Brad, mainly because Brad had no alibi for his whereabouts for the first two murders, only that he was at his studio working alone. Now at least this time he had an alibi but he still was suspicious of his actions because it really frightened him to think of Brad taking advantage of Becky at her age, but he would have to trust what Becky was telling him was the truth. He would only hope that these three incidents had scared the rest of the girls enough that they would take extra precautions.

The entire community became abuzz with the news of the third murder. For the first time the media, both the newspapers and local TV, were beginning to throw around the *serial killer* words which instilled fright into everyone. It was the last thing Lieutenant Franklin and his task force wanted introduced to the entire community so he held a news conference at noon on the next day to try to quell some of the rumors that began flying around concerning the murders. He at least had to get all the true facts out to the public.

Five days after Margy's murder, once the autopsy was complete, her funeral took place. The main focus of Lieutenant Franklin and his task force was to stay on the sidelines out of the main stream and observe everyone that attended. He was aware that many times a killer, especially a serial killer, will want to be there, not only to observe the results of his actions, but to appear to mourn the victim. But it was tough, as you can imagine just about the entire community came to the services, especially all the kids that attended high school and college with Margy. It was again a heart-wrenching day to go through; one that the entire community hoped they would never go through again.

11

Fall began to turn to winter as the first semester of school was coming to an end and Thanksgiving was right around the corner. Most of the crowd saw each other at school but consciously stayed in because of the fear that had spread throughout the community. The message to not travel around alone really hit home with everyone and rarely did you ever see any of them, especially the girls, walking or riding by themselves, especially at night.

Randy, Jennifer's old boyfriend, decided to have a party the week before Thanksgiving and spread the word to everyone. He had stayed pretty much to himself after the murders of Jennifer and Roxanne, just concentrating on football and other sports. The accusations about his secret romance with Roxanne had turned many of the girls in the crowd sour towards him, but most of them just didn't believe it or just didn't want to. Randy was a popular guy in high school, especially with the girls, and none of that popularity seemed to stop once he got into college. He just wanted to get everyone together again; it seemed that the crowd was just drifting apart so much with everything that had happened, so it was time for a party.

Everyone in their crowd attended along with a few of Randy's jock friends who brought dates. The only remaining 'couple' in the crowd was Fran and Mike who were of course closest friends to Jennifer and Randy so with Jennifer gone they hadn't seen much of Randy.

Most of the parties Randy and Jenn threw were in Randy's basement which was big enough to hold a comfortable crowd. It was completely finished, had a large brick fireplace at one end and a big screen TV and pool table at the other end. As usual, most of the girls huddled around the fireplace talking about everyone and everything while the guys congregated around the pool table.

The few times that Randy would venture out for some social life he would spend most of his time with John and Peter. The three of them pulled each other through this ordeal of losing their girlfriends to a murderer so understandably it gave the three of them a close comradery that each of them were in need of.

Of course Becky and Brad were together off and on throughout the night, trying to play the role of good friends rather than secret lovers. She looked especially beautiful tonight in a short black silky dress that clung to her body like a glove which of course was driving Brad crazy being able to see her yet not being able to touch her. What made it even worse was her flirtatious ways with him all night long, just teasing him to death with her eyes and vivacious moves. But he managed to tease her back by hanging out at the pool table with the guys trying not to give her the attention she so desired.

It was only about midnight when some of the crowd started to say goodnight and leave. Fran and Mike were first and of course most everyone knew that they wanted some alone time together. Brad was the next to leave, telling everyone he was dead tired from a long day on the job and just needed to crash at home and get some shuteye. It was everything he could do leaving Becky there as he wanted so much just to take her back to his place and explore that black silky dress, but he told her they had to continue to play their role and he would see her tomorrow night when they could have the night all to themselves. She regretfully agreed.

Stephanie and Rhonda spent the last half of the night at the pool table toying with the guys while attempting to shoot pool. Stephanie was paying special attention to Randy while Rhonda teased Billie and Peter most of the night. Randy and Stephanie had always flirted and kidded each other but just as friends, they never seemed to have the same chemistry for each other; but tonight seemed different. Stephanie's long black hair cascading over her shoulders and her low cut red sweater revealing lots of cleavage seemed to continually catch Randy's eye. It had been six long months since Jennifer's death, so neither of them felt like they had to shy away from what seemed to be happening. It wasn't long before the two of them wandered out the back sliding glass doors into the darkness of the faintly moonlit night.

"It's really great seeing you tonight Steph, I'm really glad you came," Randy said as he led her by the hand over to the hanging swing in the back yard.

"I know," she answered back, "I'm so glad I came tonight. I wasn't going to because I was afraid it would be a sad night with everyone together again without Jenn, Roxy, and Margy; but I knew it was time for all of us to move on as hard as that may be.

"Yeah that's why I decided to have the party. We've all always been so close through the years and it seems like we've just drifted apart so much since this whole thing happened. It's been six months since Jenn died and I think I'm just ready to move on with my life. Not that I'll ever forget her, but I think I've punished myself enough. Do you think I'm wrong wanting to move on?"

"No," Stephanie whispered as she held his hand and moved it to her lap. "You can't spend the rest of your life driving yourself crazy over what's happened. You lost the girl of your dreams, your soul mate, and that's not an easy thing to cope with. I mean you're only human and you have to move on with your life."

"Thanks Steph," Randy whispered back as he leaned over towards her and gently kissed her on the cheek.

As he pulled back away from her their eyes met in a passionate embrace. They were only inches apart as their eyes focused intently on each other. Her other hand moved up to the back of his head as she softly pulled him closer to her. Their lips met ever so softly as he pulled back inches apart again as his hand moved up and followed the outline of her hair down her face onto her neck. He brushed her neck with the back of his fingers as he moved his hand back up to her cheek. Brushing her cheek softly he cupped his fingers under her chin and kissed her lips again and again. His tongue traced the outline of her lips first top and then bottom. Her lips were soft and moist, natural, free of any lipstick. The force of their breath collided as they both felt a surge of heat inside of them.

"Is this okay with you?" he asked as his eyes opened and went back to her eyes.

She moved her hand from the back of his head until her fingers were gently rubbing his lips.

"Yes," she whispered, "this is absolutely okay with me. I've wanted to call you so many times just to hear your voice and to tell you that I'm here if you need to talk to anyone, but I was always afraid of being too forward or maybe you weren't ready to move on. Yes it is definitely okay with me Randy."

"It's funny," he whispered back, "we've flirted and teased each other for the past two years. You were always the bitch of the crowd and I was always the conceited boyfriend so the flirting never really meant anything because we were such close friends and we expected that from each other, but we've just grown to always play with each other in a friendly way, so maybe deep down inside it did mean something."

"Well I've always felt something for you ever since we met in high school. I used to love to come to your football games and watch you, but Jenn was one of my very best friends and I certainly would not have done anything to jeopardize my friendship with her or my friendship with you. So I guess the only way to satisfy my desires was to flirt with you and treasure our strong friendship. But now..."

"But now," he interrupted "now we have the chance to act on those flirtations and feelings. At least I'd like to."

They were still just inches apart as they continued to softly whisper to each other as if someone else could hear them.

"I'd like nothing more than to put some serious effort behind these flirtations and finally get to show you how my heart feels," her voice quivered as she finally could say those words to him. "Do you think the rest of the world is ready for us?"

"Do you care?" he answered as both of his hands wrapped tightly around her two hands.

"No, let's just do it and see what happens. But enough talk, would you please kiss me again...please."

He didn't need to be asked a second time as their lips met in a strong passionate kiss. They both wrapped their arms around each other and pulled close as their bodies touched for the first time. He was gentle at first touch, but she immediately pressed hard against him wanting to get closer and closer.

They both suddenly pulled back as the door to the basement opened as Rhonda and Billie came strolling out.

"Hey we wondered what you two were up to; we didn't realize you were out here," said Billie as he pulled out a cigarette and lit it.

"Yeah we're just getting re-acquainted with each other," Randy answered back as he got up off the swing. He pulled Stephanie up by the hand and they walked towards the door hand in hand. "I never knew you smoked. I don't think I've ever seen you smoke before. Did you just start?"

"No I've always smoked but I usually just do it in private. I know it's a nasty habit so I try not to do it when I'm with friends who don't smoke," answered Billie as he noticed the two of them coming toward them hand in hand.

"What's this?" Billie asked as he motioned towards the two of them, "are you guys an item now?"

Randy and Stephanie looked at each other with this huge smile on their faces as they both shook their heads yes.

"Yeah, we've had this chemistry between us all night long, so we talked it over and decided to give it a try," Stephanie answered with a gleam in her eye.

"Wow that's great," shouted Rhonda, "you two have been such good friends for so long I can't imagine it not working out. Congratulations."

"Thanks," said Randy, "I hope everyone has the same feelings about this that you do."

"Hey if they don't like it they can go pound sand," joked Billie as he took a last puff and crushed his cigarette on the ground. Reaching in his pocket he pulled out a pack of breath mints and popped one in his mouth. "Maybe you and I can join them and become the next new couple. What do you say, Rhonda?"

He grabbed her hand, spun her around in a dancing motion, and pulled her close to him, dipping her back towards the ground.

"You know you want me," he said as he pulled her back up towards him.

"Only if you drop that filthy smoking habit," she said as she laughed and waved her hand in front of her face as if to swat his bad breath away.

The four of them laughed as they opened the door and went back in the house to join the crowd.

Becky and Peter approached them to say goodnight and thank Randy for the party. Peter said he would give Becky a lift since Fran and Mike had left earlier and Becky came with them. Becky's house was right on the way to Peter's so she accepted the invite.

"Hey you guys leaving?" Randy asked.

"Yeah he's going to give me a ride home on his way. It's getting kind of late for me so I better head out," Becky said as she leaned forward to give Randy a peck on the cheek.

"Hey good, don't want you walking home by yourself. Take care Beck. You too Peter and thanks for coming."

"You bet," Peter answered, "see ya' at school Monday."

They all said their goodbyes as most of the remaining singles and couples gathered together to head out for the night. As Billie and Rhonda walked out they looked back at the lone remaining couple and smiled with approval.

"Don't you two do anything we wouldn't," snapped Billie as Rhonda hauled off and punched him in the arm. They walked down the sidewalk laughing and nudging each other back and forth.

As Stephanie and Randy went back in the house together, Billie and Rhonda decided to say their goodbyes for the night since it was getting late and continue their new found interests another day. Since they drove separately to the party Billie insisted on following her home and promised to call her the next day. It wasn't far to her house and as she parked on the street in back of her dad's car, Billie drove up alongside, waved goodnight, blew her a big fat kiss and then slowly drove off blinking his high beam lights as a fond farewell.

Rhonda laughed and shook her head as she gathered her purse and sweater and got out of the car, pushing the lock button on her keychain to turn on the car alarm. It was a full moon that night so it seemed much brighter to her than normal as she slowly strolled up her sidewalk to the house. Her mind was engulfed in the party and particularly in Billie and maybe what was going to happen between them.

As she got about halfway up the flower lined walkway she noticed that the porch light that her parents always left on for her was not on. There was an inside light on that she could see through the front window curtains, but it was odd, no porch light.

Just then the still of the night was interrupted by the snapping of a branch that echoed in the still night like a cannon going off. Her heart skipped a beat as she jumped to face the sound coming from the tree in the front yard. She didn't hesitate for a second as she picked up her pace heading directly to the front door, her eyes never leaving the tree as she reached the door and grabbed the knob. Her key was in the lock and the door was open in a matter of seconds as she flicked on the outside light. The brightness of the light lit up the entire front yard which was empty except for two squirrels scurrying up the trunk of the tree. She breathed a sigh of relief as she closed the door behind her, locking it, and turning off the light. Thoughts of Jennifer home alone the night of her murder crossed her mind as she put her hand to her heart as if to slow down the thumping coming from inside.

The light from the top of the stairway went on as her mother whispered hello and asked if everything was okay.

"Sure mom I'm fine...I was just scared when I didn't see the front porch light on. It wasn't like you to not have it on. I guess with everything that's happened around here lately it just freaked me out."

Her mother apologized and said they had fallen asleep watching a movie in bed and reassured her everything was okay.

The night of the full moon passed without incident as all the girls made it home safely.

12

As the holidays arrived and passed, things seemed to almost be returning to normal except for the occasional visit from Lieutenant Franklin. The murder investigation seemed to be at a standstill with no clues, no firm suspects, and nothing but frustration from the police and the community. The murderer had left completely clean crime scenes, there were no witnesses, and the rest of the kids could come up with nothing that could help the police at all.

As far as the crowd, everything had settled down and the holidays and winter break brought much joy and spirit to everyone. Stephanie and Randy were a hot item and everyone involved had been more than supportive of their newfound relationship. Rhonda and Billie were exclusively dating and not only saw each other almost every night but were taking quite a few classes together at college. Fran and Mike made it a Christmas to remember by announcing to their families that they were engaged. No wedding date had been set since they both wanted to finish college and get established in the business world before going ahead with their plans, but Becky was overjoyed at being the maid of honor to her big sister. Both she and Brad had kept their promise and kept their relationship a secret, as hard as it was, especially through the holidays as they visited each other's family. Brad was also very determined to take their relationship ever so slowly and not let Becky get carried away physically. But Becky also knew that she wanted Brad to be her date for her sister's wedding so she knew she'd have to break the news to the family in the near future.

As the holidays came to an end and the school semester started back up, winter began to rear its ugly head as snow began to fall almost every day. Maryland weather was always a challenge since each of the four seasons was so prevalent; the winters were always cold, icy, windy and snowy; the summers were hot, humid, and stormy; and the spring and fall seasons were warm and cool and absolutely beautiful, from the blooming of the flowers to the changing colors of the leaves. It was a great place to live if you wanted a little bit of everything. The motto was always 'if you're tired of the weather just wait until tomorrow, it will change'.

During part of their investigation, Lt. Franklin's team had come across one firm link between the three girls; they were all on the cheerleading team in high school. Inspector Wiley had spent a lot of time at the high school interviewing all of their teachers, counselors, and fellow students and had come up fairly empty, but then there was the cheerleading coach.

G. Lusby

"His name is Jake Bannister and he is thirty-one-years-old," said the inspector as he reviewed his notes. "He has coached the cheerleading squad at the high school for five years and before that was a gymnastics instructor. He's been teaching a total of eight years since he was twenty-three and fresh out of college. He was born and raised in Chicago and moved here to take the teaching job and has a completely clean record with nothing, not even a traffic ticket."

"No problems or complaints from any of the girls through the years," the lieutenant asked.

"No, no problems at all; in fact, quite the opposite. He's a real good-looking athletic guy and the girls absolutely love him. I went down to the football field for a couple of practices and most of time he's walking around with his arm around one of them or they're hangin' on him. He's quite the lady's man."

"Sounds a little too friendly for a school coach, doesn't it? Well let's observe him for another day or too and then question some of the girls and see if we come up with anything before we question him."

They all agreed and set Friday as the date they would get back together to review the inspector's findings, but they never made it to Friday. On Thursday morning the office received a call from the local dispatcher that a body had been found in the woods behind the school. The lieutenant and his team rushed to the scene.

They arrived in one car and could see that the area had already been taped off by the officers and no one was being allowed in until they arrived. They met with the officer who answered the dispatch call.

"Hey George, what do you have for us," asked the lieutenant.

"Good morning lieutenant. Over there in the blue t-shirt and tan shorts is the guy who discovered the body and called it in. He was jogging down the path that leads through the park over there through the wooded area and spotted the body lying between a couple of trees over there. He had his cell phone with him and called 911 right away. No one has talked to him yet."

"Thanks George. Just keep the area clean and don't let anyone in. And especially keep the media out and away from us for a while. If they give you a problem then let me know."

"Okay lieutenant."

The three of them walked over to the small stone wall that the jogger was sitting on.

"Hello, I'm Lieutenant Will Franklin and this is Inspector Tom Wiley and Inspector George Burton, we're from the homicide department."

The jogger got up and held out his hand. "Hi, my name is Ted, Ted Simms, and I discovered the body."

"Yes we know, now can you tell us exactly what happened."

"Sure. Well I jog down here every morning about this same time, about eight-thirty or so, and today I looked over as I was coming down the path and saw these two legs between the trees over there. There's usually no one else around when I jog, that's why I like to come out at this time, it's nice and quiet, no kids skating and running up and down like they always do."

"Sure, go on."

"Well, I stopped and went over and saw it was a girl so I just got on my cell phone right away and called the police. That's about it."

"Did you touch anything...like the girl or anything around her?"

"No sir, as soon as I saw her laying there with her clothes ripped off, I just came back over to the path and called."

"Did you see anyone else around during your whole jog this morning?" asked Inspector Burton.

"No sir, no one. Like I said that's why I like to jog here at this hour, it's quiet and no one else is around."

"Okay," said the lieutenant, "just give all your personal information to that officer over there so we can contact you if we need to and thanks a lot for your cooperation."

The three of them walked over to the area of trees and could see the body lying between them. She looked to be in her late teens with long blonde hair laying flat on the ground entangled with leaves and brush. Her blouse and bra were ripped open and lying off to the side, her shorts and panties were off and no where around. Her hands were bound over her head with grey duct tape which was also over her eyes and mouth and as before, there was an inscription on the duct tape in black marker that read *'I just can't help myself'*. Her legs were spread open, she had obviously been raped.

"Damn, another one. Tom, get your camera and take pictures of all of this before we touch anything."

"Sure Will," he answered as he backtracked to the car.

They took pictures of the entire crime area and her body. As they finished up the coroner arrived and upon quick examination he determined by the marks on her neck that she had been strangled and possibly raped, and estimated that she had been dead for eight to ten hours. They searched the surrounding area and did not come up with her clothes or any identification.

It would be later that afternoon before they would find out she was Christine Vicors, a senior at the high school. Her parents reported her missing late the evening before when she didn't return from visiting a friend who lived on the other side of the park. Her parents said she didn't drive, she always walked through the park and down the jogging path to get to her friend's house. The investigation revealed she left her girlfriends house at about ten-thirty Wednesday night on her way home.

She lived about five blocks from the school and didn't hang out with anyone in the crowd, in fact, none of the kids or parents even knew her, except for Becky who knew her from school. They were both seniors but weren't in any classes together, she just knew her from cheerleading.

The police station was abuzz the next morning, as was the whole town. This was the fourth murder in six months and the police were getting a lot of pressure to bring this case to resolution. The lieutenant called the entire team into the meeting room to be addressed by the chief of police.

Chief Dawson entered the room and went swiftly and directly to the podium at the front of the room.

"Okay, everyone listen up. As you can imagine I am getting immense pressure from the mayor, the community, and now the governor, to solve this case. We have four beautiful girls raped and murdered within a six month period and I need to know what we are doing about this."

Lieutenant Franklin stood up. "Well Chief, unbelievably we do not have much to go on. We are convinced by each murder scene that the girls were attacked by the same man who seems to leave us one clue at each crime scene, a message on each victim's taped mouth. The messages are 'I am so sorry', 'you are just so beautiful', 'you drive me crazy', 'I just can't help myself'. Each crime scene is wiped down clean of fingerprints, body fluids, footprints, and tire tracks, plus each body is wiped down with alcohol solution. The only visible clue at three of the four crime scenes was a cigarette butt, but unbelievably there have been no DNA traces on the first two and we're still waiting for the results from last night's murder. There have been no witnesses to any of the crimes, no substantial leads from any of the friends or relatives, and no hard and fast suspects to speak of."

"Well," the Chief commented, "this guy certainly is a tidy murderer isn't he? Do you have any suspicions on who might be involved?"

"Well yes and no. Now we haven't questioned anyone for this fourth murder last night, but there are two people we are watching intently. One is a twenty-four-year-old photographer named Brad Townsend who hangs out regularly with the nineteen-year-old crowd that has been the target of the first three murders. Then, we have one link to all four murders and that is that they all were cheerleaders at the high school and coached by Jake Bannister. He's thirty-one- years-old, has been the coach for five years and is quite the ladies man."

"Any record on either one of them?" asked the Chief.

"No sir, both clean. We've questioned Brad Townsend quite a few times but haven't approached Mr. Bannister; we've just been observing him. Now that we have a fourth murder that is outside of this particular group of kids, we'll talk to him first thing in the morning."

"Okay gentlemen, let me know of any further developments no matter how minor they are; I need to give the media and the public something to hold them off. Does anyone know about the messages left at each scene?"

"No Chief...that is except for the individuals that discovered the bodies, but so far that info has not leaked out to anyone that we are aware of. I suspect after this murder hits the papers, the word *serial* will soon be applied."

Chief Dawson agreed as he left the room shaking each of their hands as he walked past them.

"Let's not wait until the morning, let's go interview this cheerleader coach this afternoon," snapped Lt. Franklin as he slammed his notebook at his hand. "We've got to get a break soon."

The high school classes let out at two-twenty in the afternoon and football practice and cheerleading practice ran from three to four-thirty three days a week. Today was a practice day.

Lieutenant Franklin and Inspector Wiley went to the school by themselves so as not to intimidate anyone by showing up in mass. The practice was in session so they just glided into the stands sitting with the parents and kids that were watching. The football coaches had the players out on the field running passing and blocking drills, while the cheerleader coach and his assistant practiced routines on the sidelines in front of the stands.

Jake Bannister was the young good-looking athletic type with dark black hair and brown eyes. He worked closely with the girls and guys and demonstrated each routine that the guys were supposed to perform as they put their hands on the girls' waist and lifted them up over their heads. He would end each routine by tossing the girl up in the air and catching her in his outstretched arms. The girls seemed to love working with him, especially when he had them in his arms. Even when they took breaks he seemed to be surrounded by the girls as they clung ever so tightly around him.

It was almost four-thirty as we saw the football team sprint off the field and head for the locker rooms. The cheerleaders had also finished their routines and were starting to walk off the field with the coach as he had his arm around two of them as they walked.

"Ah excuse me...Coach Bannister," the lieutenant yelled, "could we possibly speak with you for a moment?"

"Sure," he yelled back as he motioned for the girls and guys to head inside for the day. "What can I do for you gentlemen?"

"Yes, if we could have a minute of your time over here by the grandstands, we'd appreciate it," said the lieutenant as he watched the other parents and kids leaving the now empty stands. "My name is Lieutenant Franklin and this is Inspector Wiley. We're from the local homicide division and we're investigating..."

The coach interrupted him. "Yes, my god, the three murders that have happened. I read about them in the papers. Tragic, tragic stories."

"Well coach, we're sorry to say the number is now at four. Last night we found the body of Christine Vicors."

The coach raised his hands to his head. "Oh my god, you're kidding me; not Christine too. She wasn't in school or at practice today so we thought she was just sick or something. Murdered! Oh God!"

"Can we ask you coach where you were last night between the hours of ten and twelve in the evening?" asked Inspector Wiley.

The coach took his hands away from his head and stared over at the two of them intently without saying a word. His stare was that of disbelief and astonishment as he seemed to be studying the words that came out of his mouth. Finally he spoke, "Where was I last night? You're asking me as if you think I had something to do with her murder. Come on guys I love these girls...these girls are my life, and have been for eight years now. Surely you can't think I had anything to do with this?"

"Mr. Bannister," the inspector continued, "we are simply performing an investigation on these murders and questioning everyone who has ever had contact with these girls. You sir, have had contact with all four of these girls at one time or another. Is that correct sir?"

"Well yes, they have all been cheerleaders on my squad. But I loved each one of them. I went to their funerals and cried just as everyone else did."

"We know, we saw you there."

"You have been watching me and suspecting me of these crimes?"

"Coach, we have been watching and observing everyone, from the parents to the friends to the classmates to the teachers, everyone. So it's not just you, so please answer the question, where were you last night?"

"Aahh let's see...last night I was...ah home. No wait, I went to eat at the Red Lobster restaurant on Midway Boulevard and then walked home."

"And what time was that sir?" asked the Inspector.

"Aahh that was about seven-thirty that I ate dinner and finished about nine or so and walked home."

"Well that seems like a pretty good walk from Midway to your house. What time did you get home?"

"I guess about ten-thirty or quarter to eleven, something like that."

"And then what did you do, did you stay home the rest of the night?"

"Well yes, I watched TV for a while, the World Series of Poker on ESPN, and then I fell asleep."

"Can anyone vouch for that coach?" the lieutenant asked.

"Well no, I was alone eating, but I have the credit card receipt to prove I was there…and let's see…I didn't really run into anyone walking home, and I live alone so, no."

"Okay, we'll check it out with the restaurant just to back you up, okay? Now, which way did you walk home?"

"Well I eat down there a lot. Ya' know there's a lot of restaurants on Midway and I eat down there alone a few times a week; so I always walk down and back pretty much the same way, down Midway to the park, through the park, down the jogging path, and through the ball fields to Crescent Drive where I live."

"You didn't see anyone during your whole walk home last night, not one soul?"

"No. Wait…I did see one guy on a bike. Yeah, he almost ran me over pedaling down the path so fast. I had to jump out of the way to keep from getting hit. I yelled at him but he just kept racing down the path."

"Which way and where?"

"Let's see...it was in the park and he was heading towards Midway, because I was walking towards the jogging path, towards home."

"Did you get a good look at him at all?"

"No, it happened so fast. I do know that he was riding a silver colored racing bike and one thing I did notice that seemed awful funny to me at the time...he was wearing dress shoes instead of tennis shoes. I mean who would ride a bike with dress shoes on. Stupid!"

"Do you remember anything else about him? Did he have a hat on, or glasses, and how about the color shirt?"

"No I didn't see his face at all, he appeared and zipped by me so fast I didn't get a look at him. From the back I could see he was wearing a ball cap, black I think, and a blue colored shirt."

"Okay coach, well thanks a lot. Could you do us a favor?"

"Sure anything."

"Could you come down to the precinct tomorrow after school, since you don't have practice on Thursdays and talk with us some more? Maybe by then you'll remember something about this guy on the bike that you forgot to tell us...okay?"

"Sure, I'll be down there about three o'clock."

"Good, see ya' then. And thanks a lot coach we appreciate your time today."

The two of them walked to their car as the coach went in the school. They agreed that maybe they had two good leads towards the murderer, the mysterious guy on the bike and the coach...the ladies man.

13

The lieutenant arrived at his office ten of eight in the morning only to find Bob and Julie Thomas sitting at his desk waiting for him.

"Mr. and Mrs. Thomas, good to see you again," he said as he reached out and shook both of their hands. "What brings you down here this early in the morning?"

Julie Thomas spoke up without giving her husband a chance.

"Lieutenant we are scared to death about these murders. We have two beautiful girls and we go crazy every time they leave the house every day."

"Let me interrupt you Mrs. Thomas…let me assure you that we are doing everything within our power to find this murderer and bring this all to an end. This last murder was not one of the girls that hung around with your daughters like the first three were, so we're following up a lot of leads right now. I know the thought of this whole thing is driving you crazy and I can't blame you, I have two daughters of my own."

Bob Thomas jumped in. "With all due respect lieutenant, your kids aren't teenage girls that are under attack every day with this madman out there. Both Fran and Becky are scared to death to even go to sleep at night."

"I understand that sir, and I assure you, as long as they conduct themselves like we outlined for you at the meeting two weeks ago, they will be safe. As long as they don't travel alone and use common sense, they should have no problem. Killers like this never attack when there are multiple people around, they concentrate purely on the lone victim in a secluded area. Now please folks, go home and assure your girls that they will be safe if they do as we ask."

"Okay lieutenant, thanks, and we're sorry to bother you, but..."

"No buts Mr. Thomas, I understand. Just tell your girls to use their heads and travel together. Does Becky still see Brad Townsend a lot?"

"Well yes," she answered, "surely you don't still suspect him of this?"

"No ma'am I don't really suspect him of anything, I just don't know much about him and he is twenty-four-years-old and she's sixteen. That's all, just a little scary thinking about that age difference."

"Believe me lieutenant," Mr. Thomas assured him, "if we had any doubts or suspicions of Brad in the least, we would forbid Becky to be with him alone, but he is a very fine young man and a professional and seems to just have Becky's career in mind. I'll definitely go down this afternoon and have a good talk with him anyway...but we really do trust him."

"Well, whatever makes you comfortable, that's all that counts."

They shook hands and left the room just as the two other inspectors entered the office. The lieutenant briefed them on the conversation he had just had as the three of them prepared to get the interview room ready for the coach's arrival.

"I want to hit this guy hard when we get him in here and see if we can break him early. I just have a sneaky suspicion that this guy loves his *girls* just a little too much," he said as he motioned for them to follow him into the room.

The interview with Coach Bannister went as planned as the three detectives hammered at him for two straight hours. They shoved pictures of the four pretty girls at him, and then followed that up with the four gruesome photographs of the murdered victims. He was asked to come up with his whereabouts and alibi's for the four nights in question and provided very little substantial information since again, he lives and travels very much alone. The coach defended his conduct with all of his girls and relied heavily on his clean record and flawless conduct in school. The detectives had no recourse but to ease off and let him go.

It was about two weeks later while going down to the ball fields to candidly observe the coach at one of his practices that Inspector Burton ran into Brad in the stands watching the practice.

"Hey Brad, surprised to see you down here in the middle of the afternoon. Isn't this a work day for you?"

"Well, I guess it is Inspector, but ya' know, when you run your own business you can make your own hours," Brad said laughingly. "I knock off early a lot of times and come down to take pictures of Becky at practice."

The inspector looked around on both sides of Brad. "I don't see any camera equipment to take pictures with."

"Yeah, my camera stuff is in my car over there. I came down late today and wasn't sure I'd make it in time to take pictures."

"Oh okay. By the way Brad, I've been thinking about getting some pictures taken of my kids...you know, some professional pictures, and I thought maybe I could stop by your place one day and see some of your work."

"Sure, just stop down anytime, I'd be glad to show you. In fact, I'll show you Becky's portfolio and you can see why we're together so much," Brad said as he gave the inspector a judgmental look and a smirky smile.

Two days would pass before the lieutenant could follow up on his promise to Brad, which was obviously a ploy just to get to him for some additional questioning. Brad was taken by surprise as the lieutenant entered the studio to find him just coming out of the dark room.

"Hey lieutenant, I thought maybe you forgot about stopping down. In fact I really didn't expect to see you at all; truthfully I thought you were just making conversation with me that day at the ball field."

"No," answered the lieutenant, "I really am considering getting some professional pictures taken and the word around town is that you are pretty good at what you do. You really do have a real nice setup here."

"Well, it's not the best studio or best equipment that you'll ever see, but it does the trick for now. Someday I'll have the very best, someday...but until then I do the best I can with what I have. Let me show you some sample pictures over here...and we'll start out with Becky's portfolio that I told you about.

Lieutenant Franklin sat down at the cutting table that was in the center of the room and began to slowly leaf through the album. Brad watched over his shoulder for a few minutes, commenting on different pictures and various poses, before saying, "I'll be right back, I have some strips of film processing in the dark room and I'll just be a few minutes finishing them up."

"Sure thing, no rush," he answered as he watched Brad go in and close the door. He looked around the studio, which was half neatly arranged, and the other half hidden behind a standing screen which blocked off the cluttered half. It was obvious which half was used for entertaining prospective clients and which half was a work in progress. Looking over towards the closed darkroom door he stepped behind the screen and began to look around on the cluttered side. There were boxes and boxes of new film, new light fixtures, light bulbs and accessories and against the wall were three or four rolled up background screens that were used as backdrops for portraits. As he leaned over to pull out one of the screens to look at the background color, he noticed a crumpled up paper bag that had small drops of what looked like blood on it that was pushed back behind the rolled up backdrops. He took a handkerchief out of his pants pocket and slowly and quietly pulled the bag out from behind the drops and opened it. Looking inside he could see what seemed to be a woman's skirt and panties, also with some blood on them. He carefully rolled the bag up tight and carried it back to the table where he had been sitting. His assumption was that these were the missing clothes from the Christine Vicors murder.

Moments later Brad returned from his dark room chores and the lieutenant directed his attention to the bag.

"Brad, can you tell me what this is that I found in your room over there?"

Brad looked puzzled but nervous as he walked over to the bag. "I have no idea, where did you get it?"

"I was looking at your background screens over in the corner there and saw this tucked in behind them. Kind of looks like blood drops to me."

"I honestly have no idea lieutenant; I don't think I've ever seen that bag before. What's inside?" Brad asked as he reached over and grabbed a cigarette out of the pack sitting on the desk behind him.

"Clothes," he answered, "woman's clothes."

Brad lit his cigarette with a lighter he pulled out of his pants pocket. "Lieutenant, I have never seen that bag before in my life."

"Well then, with your permission, I'm going to take the bag with me and have our folks take a look at it."

"Sure."

"Okay, good, I'll take it with me, but let me tell you something Brad. If this turns out to be what I think it is, it's not going to look real good finding it here. So I'm asking you to stay in the area and not leave town until I get back to you. I don't like what I see here, but I'm going to give you the benefit of the doubt and take your word that you will not leave town...okay."

"You got it lieutenant, I have nothing to hide and no reason to leave town. What do you think it is?"

"I'd rather not say just yet, but I'll get back to you tomorrow."

With that, he picked up the bag, again using the handkerchief, and walked out of the studio to his car. The adrenalin was pumping through his body as he hoped this was the break they had been waiting for. As he drove away he made a call on his cell phone to the precinct and had a squad car sent to the area to watch over Brad and make sure he didn't wander away too far. On one side he wanted this to be the break they had been waiting for, and on the other hand he hoped for Becky's sake that he was wrong. He took everything straight to the lab and ordered a complete analysis as quickly as possible.

It only took twenty-four hours for the top priority analysis to be complete and the finding was that the clothes and blood definitely without a doubt were from the victim Christine Vicors. He also got a call from the lab that the cigarette butt found at the scene of the last murder had traces of DNA on it and it proved to be a perfect match with Brad. He called the patrol car stationed outside of Brad's studio and told them to arrest Brad and bring him to the station immediately.

14

The lieutenant and both Inspectors lined the outside of the questioning room as Brad was brought in and sat down at the table in the center of the room.

Lieutenant Franklin spoke first. "Brad, first I'll ask you straight up. Did you rape and kill these four girls?"

The pictures of the four murdered girls were lying on the table top in front of Brad.

"No I did not. I have said it before and I'll say it again lieutenant, I did not commit any crime."

The two Inspectors each pulled a chair to each side of Brad and at that point began drilling him with facts and questions. They relayed the fact that the clothes of the fourth murdered girl were found in his studio in a bag that had her blood on it; they were very suspicious of his lack of alibis for two of the four murders; and his brand of cigarette was found at two of the four murder scenes with his DNA on the cigarette.

Brad continued to deny any involvement with any of the crimes and claimed that the bag and cigarette must have been planted there by the real killer.

"Well if that's the case," asked the lieutenant, "then who could it be? Has anyone broken into your studio in the past week?"

"No, not that I'm aware of," answered Brad. "Can I smoke in here?"

"Sure. Okay, no break-ins. So how about visitors; who has been to see you in the past few days at the studio?"

Brad puffed on his cigarette as he rubbed his forehead with his other hand. "Let's see...Becky has been down a couple of times...almost every day in fact. And...her dad stopped down yesterday afternoon to talk with me, and her sister and mom were in the day before to talk to me about taking Fran's wedding pictures. And...a few other customers that were looking into hiring me. I can get their names for you if you want; I have them written down at the studio."

"You didn't know any of them before they came in?"

"No...well wait a minute...yes I did. There was Mr. Marshall, Billy Marshall's dad who wanted some family pictures taken; and Coach Bannister from the high school stopped by to see if I could take some pictures of the whole cheerleading squad after practice one day; and I think that's it."

The three investigators immediately looked at each other as they heard the coach's name mentioned.

"Let me ask you Brad, did any of your visitors bring anything into the studio with them when they visited? Now think hard, this could be very important for you."

Brad continued to take drags of his cigarette as he rubbed his forehead and thought about the question. "Well yes, all of the ones I mentioned did. Mr. Thomas had his briefcase from work; Mrs. Thomas and Fran both had bags with samples of dresses in them to show me their colors in the wedding; Billy's dad also had a briefcase because I can remember him opening it to get out one of his business cards to give to me; and Coach Bannister had a duffel bag that he brought right from school with him."

"Brad, now think hard, do you remember leaving any of them alone when they were there to visit you?"

Brad reached over and put his cigarette out in the ash tray and started twirling the ashtray around as he thought about the question. "Well, in fact I think I left the room at one time or another with all of them. Except Billie's dad, he was only there for about five minutes and I don't remember leaving the room with him there."

"Were you gone long with the others?"

"No, not a real long time. I just went in the dark room for a minute or two when Franie and her mom were here, to get my latest negatives of Becky to show them. Then for Fran's dad, after we talked for a few minutes he asked me to get a bag out of his car that Mrs. Thomas had sent over with samples of their invitations for me to take shots of for the album cover."

"What about Jake Bannister?"

"Oh yeah, like I said, he stopped by to ask me to take some group shots of the girls after school one day next week. Yeah, he asked me if I had any shots of the team from previous years and I had to go up to my apartment upstairs to get my portfolio album. I have a bunch of pictures in there as samples."

The lieutenant had no choice but to book Brad on suspicion of murder and advise him to get legal representation immediately. They could swallow the fact that maybe the bag had been planted, because why would Brad hide the bag of clothes in his own studio; but the DNA on the cigarette butt found at the crime scene was the determining factor.

After he was booked and led away, the three investigators continued to talk over the information Brad had given them.

"Well I guess any one of them could have carried the bag into his studio," said Inspector Wiley. "Well except Mrs. Thomas and her daughter who he said had wedding clothes in their bag."

"Right," agreed the lieutenant. "Now Mr. Thomas carried a briefcase, so I guess he could have had it tucked inside. Has he had an alibi for each of the murders?"

"Well yes and no," answered Inspector Burton. "For three of the four murders he was at his office and called home from there on one of the nights. We verified that with the phone company. Other than that no one was there with him to vouch for that. On the Margy McNichol murder he was coming back from the airport after a business trip and his wife called him on his cell phone to tell him about the murder. He went right over to the McNichol's house from the airport to see them and see if there was anything he could do for them. That's all we have for him."

"Okay and we all know about Mr. Bannister," the lieutenant said as he got his notepad out of his coat pocket and flipped open the pages. "He was at home or out jogging on every single night. No alibis at all. Let's talk to both of them again and see if we can get any more information out of them."

"Both of them?" asked Inspector Burton.

"Yeah, Thomas and Bannister; let's just talk to both of them, just to cover all bases."

The next day the two inspectors split up and each questioned the two men in question. Inspector Wiley reported that after talking to Mr. Thomas at his office that day, he had no new evidence or suspicions to speak of. Mr. Thomas was very defensive about being questioned again and asked why they weren't spending more time finding the criminals rather than questioning the parents. When asked about the visit to Brad's studio, he said he didn't remember visiting him at all. Inspector Burton reported that Coach Bannister cooperated fully and quoted the same story about his visit to Brad's studio that Brad had.

It didn't take long for word to spread around town, and especially to Becky, that Brad had been arrested for suspicion of murder. She burst in the house from school with tears running down both cheeks as she sobbed out loud.

"Becky dear, what is the matter," her mother asked as she ran to the front door in horror.

"Mom," Becky said between gasps of breath, "they've arrested Brad for the murders. Can you believe they suspect Brad of doing something like that? If they knew him they'd know how silly that is."

"Now, now sweetie, everything will be alright, just you wait and see," her mother said convincingly as she hugged her and stroked her hair.

"But how could they possibly think that mom?"

"Well Becky, from what I've heard on the news today, they have arrested him because they found suspicious evidence in his studio."

"What kind of evidence?"

"Well they're not exactly saying at this point, but what they did find had Margy's blood on it, plus they've made some kind of DNA match on something. I don't know sweetie, they just don't say much on the news, just that he's being held on suspicion of murder."

"Well can't you or Dad do something to help Brad...I mean you know what kind of person he is; you've both known him for well over a year now and you know the way he treats me. He wouldn't hurt anyone. Mom we've got to do something!"

"I don't think there's anything we can do Becky, but I certainly talk it over with your father when he comes home. I'm sure he's probably heard about it on the news by now, so we'll see what he says...okay?"

The rest of the afternoon meandered by as Becky spent it in her room watching the news to get the latest reports first hand. By five-thirty she heard the front door shut which she knew meant her dad was home from work. She went running out of her room and down the steps to meet him.

"Dad, Dad, I'm so glad you're home," Becky yelled as she met up with him in the hallway on the way to the kitchen. She threw her arms around his neck as involuntary tears again began to come down her cheeks.

"Well, I've never had a greeting like this before when I arrived home. I'm glad to see you too Becky," her father answered as he embraced her hug, then pulled away as he noticed her tears. "What's the matter sweetie?"

"Dad, have you heard about Brad?" she asked.

"Yes I did sweetie, and I was very surprised and very saddened to hear about the arrest," her father said as her mother joined them in the hallway.

"She thinks we should all do something to help him clear his name," voiced her mother.

"Dad we have to. I mean like I was saying to Mom, we've all known him for well over a year now and look how many times we've been with him and he's an awesome guy. Please Dad."

"Becky, you know I hate to see you like this and I would do anything in the world for you, but I don't think it's our place to get in the middle of this investigation. Believe me, the police know what they're doing and if Brad is innocent they will find that out and release him."

"Oh please dad, we've got to come to his defense, please?"

"No Becky I don't want to get in the way of this investigation, but I'll tell you something between the three of us. I don't have any idea what they have found that is causing them to arrest him, but I will say that the police department and everyone involved is under an extreme amount of pressure to find who is doing these crimes. Now up to this point they have come up completely empty and have no leads in this crime wave, so they are desperate to give at least something positive to their superiors and to the public. I think Brad is that something that may take a little bit of pressure off of the lieutenant so they can continue on with their investigation without their brass breathing down his neck. So, let's just give them a little time and I'm sure Brad will be released and his name cleared."

"Okay Dad, I understand what you are saying, but I just can't stand to imagine him sitting in a jail cell and not being able to see him."

Her mom and dad kind of sharply looked at each other as they quickly turned back to Becky.

"Becky is there something going on between you and Brad that we don't know about?" her mom questioned.

"Maybe!" Becky answered.

16

Fran's mind was racing with excitement as she thought about all the plans her and Mike had accomplished at his house tonight. The wedding was something he hardly ever wanted to talk about, she figured it was just a guy thing, but tonight he was all lovey-dovey and even suggested moving the date up and getting married before they finished college. The decision was to think about it, but the thought of his excitement to want to marry her even sooner just drove her crazy. She couldn't wait to tell her mom.

It was a windy stormy-looking night as she pulled into the driveway and headed for the front door. It hadn't rained yet but the smell of a big storm was in the air as the trees out front swayed side to side in answer to the force of the wind. It had been an especially hot day so the cooling breeze felt good to the skin as she looked up at the moon and the approaching storm clouds in the distance. As she approached the front door a rumble of thunder in the distance caused her to flinch, turning in the direction of the sound she witnessed a flash of lightning bolt across the sky leading the way to yet another rumbling to come.

As she started to turn back towards the door and reach for the doorknob she was suddenly grabbed from behind and within a second a hand was over her mouth. She was pulled back hard against someone's body as a piece of duct tape was slapped on her eyes before she could even think what was happening to her.

She was being dragged to the side of the house away from the driveway when a huge crash echoed in the sky sending streaks of light that lit up the entire area as the sky erupted flooding the ground with rain.

As the rain began, she was thrown to the ground by her assailant and the sound of the turbulent downpour drowned out all other sounds as she lay on the ground screaming. When no one stopped her screaming she knew he must have fled as she reached up ripping the tape off of her eyes. She looked around and she was alone.

Fran continued to look around in horror as she got off the ground and went running for the front door of the house. She threw the door open as her screams now echoed in through the foyer.

"Help me, help me," she screamed as within seconds Becky came running down from her upstairs bedroom.

"Fran what's the matter?" she yelled as her feet took two steps at a time to reach the bottom. By the time she hit the final step her mother was running in from the kitchen and her dad was racing up the steps from the basement.

"Franie," her mom yelled, "what is it dear, are you okay?"

"I was attacked out front," she gasped as she tried desperately to control her breathing but the panic had control of her. "I was coming to the front door and someone grabbed me from behind and pulled me to the side of the house."

With that slight description her dad immediately ran over to the opened door and out into the rain. His journey took him completely around the house searching for anyone or anything that could give a clue as to what had happened to his daughter.

By the time he returned to the doorway and entered the foyer they had moved to the kitchen. Fran was sitting on a kitchen chair as Becky was drying her off with a towel and hugging her to calm her down while her mom was dialing 9-1-1 and asking that officers come to the house immediately.

"Did you see anything dear?" their mom said as she hung up the phone and went back over to Fran.

"No, nothing," he answered as he stood in the floor dripping wet from head to toe. "Are you alright sweetheart?" he asked as he went over to Fran and knelt down beside her with his hand on her head.

"Yes Dad," she sobbed as she continued to shake with fear over the incident.

"Did you see who it was?"

"No Dad, he put tape over my eyes as soon as he grabbed me, I couldn't see a thing."

Assured that Fran was okay, her dad got back up and again went out the front door and to the side of the house looking for the tape and any other clues he could find in the pouring rain.

Returning inside, he handed the rain-soaked piece of tape to their mother as Becky came over and began wiping the water off of her father.

"Here's the tape he used, but I didn't see anything else...it's raining cats and dogs out there."

The four of them had hardly absorbed what had happened before they turned looking down the hallway at two police officers standing in the still opened front doorway.

"Hello, Mr. and Mrs. Thomas," they asked as they slowly entered the house, "you called 9-1-1?"

"Yes come in officers," he answered as he walked towards them holding out his hand. "I'm Bob Thomas and this is my wife Julie and our two daughters Fran and Becky."

They shook hands as the officers followed him back into the kitchen.

"My wife called 9-1-1 because my daughter Fran just got attacked by a man in front of our home. She was coming home and..."

"Mr. Thomas," the officer interrupted, "can we let your daughter tell us what happened."

"Oh sure."

"Fran," said the officer as he knelt on one knee beside her chair, "first, are you alright? Do you need medical attention in any way?"

"No sir," she answered, "I'm fine now."

"Okay Fran, I'm Officer Jerald and this is Officer Hickens and we're here to help you in any way we can. So why don't you just tell us what happened, and just take your time, okay?"

Fran took a sip of the juice her mom had poured for her.

"I was coming home from my fiancée's house and walked to the front door to come in. I hesitated a second because the storm was stirring up and the thunder and lightning was awesome. I just turned from looking at the sky when someone grabbed me from behind and pulled me close to them. Before I could even scream they had their hand over my mouth and tape over my eyes. They pulled me to the side of the house and before I knew it they threw me to the ground and were gone."

"How did you know they were gone?"

"Well, once they threw me to the ground I listened and all I could here was the sound of the pouring rain, so I started screaming and pulled the tape off of my eyes. No one was there so I ran into the house."

"Why do you think he threw you to the ground so fast, did you do something to make him mad?"

"No, not that I know of. Maybe he saw somebody coming up the street or maybe he just got mad because it started raining so hard."

"Okay Fran, you just rest a minute and catch your breath," the officer said as he got up off his knee and joined her parents at the kitchen counter.

"Let's just let her rest a few minutes folks, she's been through quite an ordeal so she just needs to catch her breath and feel safe. Now I take it neither of you witnessed what happened or heard anything?"

"No we were both in the house; in fact all three of us were home. Where were you two?'" he asked as he looked at his wife and daughter.

"Becky was upstairs in her room and I was in the kitchen getting ready to start dinner when we heard the door fly open and Fran screaming."

"And where were you Mr. Thomas?"

"I was in the basement straightening up my workbench when I heard all the commotion upstairs. As soon as I heard screaming I came running."

"Did either of you go outside where it happened?"

"Yes, I did," he answered. "Once I heard Fran's story I ran out and around the house to see if I could spot anyone nearby or running, but nothing, it was just raining too hard to see anything."

"That's all you did outside?"

"Well no, I went back out a second time when Franie told us that they had put tape over her eyes and I found the tape she had ripped off. It was lying in the side yard. We have it right here."

Mrs. Thomas reached over and handed the tape to the officers.

"Thank you," he said, "but I wish you two wouldn't have touched the tape. I was hoping to get some prints off of it."

"Sorry," she said as she still held it out, "but we thought maybe it would blow away or get too drenched in the rain. Sorry."

"That's fine," he answered as he motioned for her to just lay it back on the countertop. "I'll make a call to our crime lab."

"Are you going to call Lieutenant Franklin from homicide?" Mrs. Thomas asked.

"Why do you think we should?"

"Because of all the murders we've had in the past few months and this obviously was the same guy since he taped her eyes shut with duct tape like the others," Mr. Thomas answered.

"Okay, we'll put a call into him also. Now relax folks and just tend to your daughter. We'll take a look around the neighborhood and be right back, okay?"

They agreed, as their attention turned back to their daughters.

17

The rain had finally let up when Lieutenant Franklin arrived accompanied by both inspectors that were also on the case. The three of them walked in the half-opened door and spotting the family in the kitchen, proceeded back to greet them.

"Is everyone okay?"

"Sure Lieutenant, Fran is fine, we're all okay now."

"Good, I'm glad to hear that. Now I spoke with the two officers out front and they told me everything that happened tonight but I have a few more questions if that's okay with you Fran?"

"Sure, I'm fine now."

"Okay, now when you left your car and walked toward the house I assume you didn't notice anything peculiar or see anyone around. Is that correct?"

"Correct, everything seemed fine except I admit I was mostly concentrating on the storm clouds and the sound of all the thunder."

"You said you were on the porch getting ready to open the door and were grabbed from behind, correct?"

"Yes."

"Now did you hear anyone walking or running up behind you as you reached for the door?"

"No, I assume they were hiding behind the big bushes on each side of the porch because I didn't hear anything except the thunder and the wind blowing the trees."

"I've asked you a hundred times to trim those bushes down Todd," her mother interjected into the conversation.

"Did he say anything at all to you?" continued the lieutenant.

"Nothing, he just grabbed me, put his hand over my mouth, pulled me against him, and covered my eyes with the tape."

"Did you try to hit or kick him?"

"No, it just happened so fast and before I knew it he threw me to the ground and was gone," she answered as she began to softly sob.

"Okay Fran that's fine, that's enough for now."

He patted Fran on the head and walked over to the kitchen counter bending down to look at the piece of weathered tape lying there. Bob and Julie Thomas followed him.

"Sorry about that Lieutenant, I just was afraid it would blow away and be lost forever."

"That's okay Mr. Thomas, I understand your intentions. Who touched the tape after you brought it in?"

"Well, unfortunately I think all of us did."

The lieutenant turned to his fellow investigators and told them both to begin canvassing the houses in the area to see if anyone spotted anything in the past hour or so. They left as he pulled out a kitchen chair and sat down.

"Don't you think it sounds like the same guy?" Mr. Thomas asked.

"Well, it's kind of early to tell except for the fact that he's in this neighborhood attacking a girl in the same crowd and he uses tape over the eyes. That's about all that we have."

Becky spoke up. "Well if it's the same guy with the same characteristics then that means it can't be Brad, right?"

"Well you're sure right Becky and I think that kind of adds even more to our current thinking."

"What's that?" Becky asked as she walked closer into the conversation.

"We have been on the verge of letting Brad free."

"Really?"

"Yes Becky, really. We've come up with some more evidence that supports Brad's theory that someone planted the items."

"Can you tell us about the evidence?" Mrs. Thomas asked.

"Yes. We went back to Brad's studio two days after he was arrested to conduct a search of the premises to see if we could spot any more clues. In that investigation we found that the back door to his studio had been forced open and the lock busted. It definitely looked like forced entry. In questioning Brad he stated he never parks out back so he never uses the back door, he always enters through the front of the studio. So, that supports his theory that someone broke in and planted the bag of clothing. And second, the cigarette butt we found at the crime scene that had Brad's DNA on it was put out with his hand not with his foot."

"What do you mean?"

"Well usually when a smoker is finished with a cigarette outside, they will throw it to the ground and step on it to put it out, thereby flattening it. That is how we found the other cigarette butts at the other crime scenes. But this butt was put out by hand. Looking in Brad's studio we could see his ash tray on his desk full of cigarettes crushed with fingers in a squeezing down motion, not flat. So, with those two facts and what happened here tonight, I think that raised enough doubt to release Brad from custody."

An instant smile came to Becky's face. "I knew it!"

"But let me tell you one thing young lady, and I hope your parents will back me up here, I want you to stay away from him, we still don't know for sure."

"But I can't stay away from him, he's my friend and..."

"That's enough Becky," her father interrupted. "As long as we are not absolutely sure who this killer is, I want both of you girls to stay as close to home as possible."

"But Dad, I *was* close to home and look what happened," replied Fran.

"I know, I know. All I'm saying is stay here as much as you can until this guy is caught. If you have to see your friends then have them over here to the house. Understood?"

They both shook their heads in agreement. Becky knew this was not the time to defend Brad and put their relationship in any more jeopardy, so she nodded and kept quiet. She knew she'd see Brad.

18

It was an especially hot day and Stephanie and Randy had just pulled up to the school parking lot to pick up her little sister Megan from cheerleading practice. Practice was about half-an-hour from ending and Stephanie wanted to be sure to be there early so Megan wasn't standing around alone waiting. The last thing she wanted was her fourteen-year-old sister telling their mom that she had to stand around and wait because Stephanie was with Randy.

As they started to get out of his convertible Stephanie noticed that practice was already over and she didn't notice her sister in the crowd of girls headed back to the gym building.

She yelled to the coach as he slowly walked behind the girls. "Hey coach, over here, it's Stephanie Hampton, remember me?"

Coach Bannister turned in the direction of the voice and held his hand over his eyes to block out the sun. He didn't respond but just started walking in the direction towards Stephanie and Randy. About halfway to the parking lot he realized who they were.

"Stephanie Hampton and Randy Bigby, what a surprise, how are you both doing?" he asked as he met them and extended his hand to Randy.

They shook hands and he turned to Stephanie and gave her a big coach bear hug.

"Now I certainly remember those big hugs of yours," Stephanie replied back as she stared into his big blue handsome eyes. Seeing him up close brought back all the memories of cheerleading practice as each of the girls eagerly awaited their turn to be near the coach.

The coach laughed. "Yes I do give big hugs, always have, and always will, that's just what I do. Stephanie you look beautiful, how long has it been?"

"I've been out of high school for two years now and I'm attending the local college here in town, but I remember seeing you at one or two of the funerals in town."

"Ah yes, the funerals, such a sad, sad time for all of us in this town to see those lovely, lovely girls just struck down by some maniac. I can't believe they haven't caught him yet. Anyway, what brings you two out here to the school today?"

"We came out to pick up my sister Megan but I didn't see her heading back to the gym."

"Well she wasn't at practice. I thought she was out sick today since the other girls said they hadn't seen her in school today."

"You're kidding me?"

"Nope, haven't seen her. I guess by your reaction she didn't stay home sick."

"No, in fact she has left for school earlier than usual the past four or five mornings because she had a report due and wanted to stop by the library and use some reference materials."

"Does she take the bus?"

"No, she usually catches a ride with two other juniors who pick her up at the house, Debbie Smith and Carolyn Fisher, but she called them last week and told them she was going in early all this week so not to pick her up."

"How was she planning on getting to school?"

"It's too late for my dad and too early for my mom so Megan said she would just leave earlier and walk, we only live about two miles from school, so she said it was no big deal."

"Well if I were you I'd let your parents know real quick. Do you know which way she would have walked to school?"

"Sure, the quickest way is through the woods down the jogging path."

"Well that goes right past my house. What time did you say she left for school?"

"I guess it was about six-fifteen this morning."

"Well I leave the house at six-forty so that I'm here at school by seven and I didn't see anyone on the path this morning at all. Anyway, I'd tell your parents immediately."

"Okay coach, thanks."

"See ya' coach, thanks," said Randy as they again shook hands.

They jumped into the front seat of the convertible, both with a serious solemn look on their face.

"Randy, I'm scared," Stephanie said as she looked over at him with a small tear already running down her cheek.

"Me too," he answered as he started the car and they sped through the parking lot. "Let's head over to your house to make sure she hasn't been home today."

She didn't answer him, her mind was running in circles fearing the worse but hoping for a positive outcome.

As they pulled up to the house Stephanie noticed that her mom's car was home but not her dad's, which wasn't unusual for this time of day.

Stephanie entered the house calling her sister's name. "Megan are you here...Megan?"

Her mom met her in the kitchen. "Megan's not here Stephanie, she hasn't come home from practice yet...in fact, you were supposed to pick her up today."

"I know mom, and Randy and I were just over there and they said Megan wasn't in school today."

"Are you sure sweetie?"

"Mom, why else do you think I'd be running in the house screaming her name. She wasn't in school today. I talked to Coach Bannister and that's what he said."

Just then the front door opened and in walked her dad.

"Jack, Megan didn't show up at school today and we don't know where she is."

He dropped his brief case by the front door and came into the kitchen to join them.

"We just went over school to pick her up after cheerleading practice and Coach Bannister told us she wasn't there today," said Randy, filling him in as quickly as possible.

"Have you talked to any of her friends?" asked her father.

"No Dad, we came right here from the practice field and all the girls had left already so we just took coach's word for it. He said the other girls told him Megan wasn't in school today, so he told us to come right home and let you both know."

"Well I'm not fooling around with this; I'm calling the police right now."

He snapped Lieutenant Franklin's card off of the refrigerator and dialed the number. He was told that the lieutenant wasn't there but they would page him and have him return the call. The good thing about the lieutenant and the good thing about living in a small college town was that everything and everyone is usually close by. Within fifteen minutes there was a knock at the door announcing the arrival of the lieutenant.

They all filled him in as to the current situation whereas he immediately made a few calls to alert his fellow officers.

"Okay, I've put out an alert for everyone to look for her, so all the patrol cars will be combing the area. Now, if I may ask, why in the world would you allow your daughter to walk to school alone at six in the morning through the woods, with everything that has been going on in this town?"

Lieutenant Franklin had a stern scolding look on his face as he posed the question to Jack and Hilary Hampton.

"I know lieutenant, it seems really stupid, but we made sure she had her cell phone and it's only two miles..."

"Only two miles? My god folks, Fran Thomas was attacked last week right at her own front door. What are you thinking?"

This time they had no answer for him. They just looked at each other and shook their heads.

"Alright, I want you Mrs. Hampton to get on the phone and call every one of her friends to see if they have seen her today. Have you tried her cell phone?"

They all looked at each other.

"No," said Stephanie, "I'll try right now." She reached in her purse, took out her own cell phone, and punched a few numbers.

All eyes were on her as she listened to the phone ringing.

Finally Megan's voice mail picked up the call, instructing the caller to leave a message.

"No, it rang, but no one answered."

"Okay," the lieutenant instructed, "while you're calling her friends I'm going to retrace her steps through the woods to the school. Now here is my cell number, if you find out anything call me immediately."

"I'll go with you lieutenant," said her father.

"No sir, you stay here at the house with your family. Randy, will you go with me?"

"Sure lieutenant, I know exactly the way she would have gone; I've walked that route myself a few hundred times."

They left out the front door as Stephanie and her parents frantically grabbed their telephone directory and began making calls.

Lieutenant Franklin and Randy left the house together, walking across the street and down the sidewalk for about four blocks then made an immediate left for about another three blocks.

"This whole thing scares me lieutenant, I'm afraid it's not going to have a happy outcome. I keep thinking of Jennifer."

"I know Randy, whenever anyone is reported missing in this town lately I get real scared too, but let's keep our fingers crossed; it's only been hours since she was seen, so maybe there's an explanation."

The wooded area could be seen behind the last three houses on the block and jutted out to the street just before the last house which was Coach Bannister's. The entrance to the jogging path was about ten feet down just beyond where the city sidewalk ended with the woods continuing beyond that and cutting across to meet the dead-end road.

Nestled in amongst the trees the coach's house seemed separated from the other houses by the woods that jutted out to the street on both sides keeping it not only alone but very quaint. As they walked past the mailbox which read *COACH*, the small one-story bungalow with white siding and dark green shutters sat in the center of a fairly well-manicured lawn and garden that formed a perfect square as it cut into the massive woods. At the far back corner of the woods sat a medium-size outdoor shed that matched the house exactly with its white siding and green trim while a basketball pole and net decorated the empty driveway.

"Must be nice to live at the end of a dead-end street like this, not much traffic to deal with," said the lieutenant.

"Probably a lot of foot traffic though, this is a real popular jogging path for everyone and a great shortcut to the school" answered Randy.

They walked past the house turning left down the jogging path that led into the woods and immediately felt cooling relief as they entered under the trees that blocked all signs of the heat of the hot day. The path was about four feet wide and had been black-topped about three years ago at the persistent request of the many bikers that use the trail. It was a windy trail that meandered to the right and back to the left around giant oak trees that seemed to create an obstacle course through the woods.

They slowly walked the trail looking from side to side at the area that surrounded them, not saying a word, just studying the lay of the land filled with leaves, brush and fallen branches. It took them about fifteen minutes to walk the entire path as they exited the woods at the edge of the school parking lot.

"Well, that's it," said Randy. "That's the way Megan would have walked to school every day this week. I mean, I assume that's how she would have walked, she'd be crazy to walk through the woods and not use the path...I can't imagine her doing that, or why she would."

"I can't either, but I'll have my men comb the woods on both sides of the path, from the coach's house clear down here to the school. For now, let's just walk back and see if we spot anything in this direction, okay?"

Randy agreed and their walk back was uneventful.

19

It was the ever so slight sign of drag marks in the dirt that led the lieutenant directly to the wooden shed in Coach Bannister's back yard.

The lieutenant had asked Randy to head on back to Stephanie's house and he would be along shortly, he wanted to canvass the area just a little bit more. He had placed a call to his fellow investigators and began walking back up the street following the outline of the woods. As he reached the sidewalk he decided to just follow the wood line behind the coach's house to continue his search. It was then that he spotted the unmistakable markings in the dirt that led out of the woods and towards the wooden shed.

As he bent down he could see that a branch of leaves had been used to smear the dirt back and forth in an attempt to cover the markings underneath. Those markings were clearly those of two feet being dragged along the ground behind a set of shoeprints.

He carefully followed those smeared markings to the front doors of the shed.

Carefully positioning his own feet he reached over with a handkerchief covering his hand and unlatched the shed door letting it swing open. Lying on the shed floor was the body of Megan Hampton.

Lieutenant Franklin had children of his own, a twelve and fourteen-year-old daughter, so everything about this murder case hit him especially hard. He caught himself so many times just sitting at home in his den staring at his two girls as they watched TV or sat studying their schoolwork. A tear would always come to his eye as he imagined that something terrible could possibly happen to one of them, a result of this bruttle animal that was terrorizing their town. He had worked on the homicide squad for the past ten years, so this was all too familiar to him, but this particular case was so brutal and so close to home that he just couldn't keep it from getting personal. He knew he would again have to face yet another set of parents, telling them the god-awful truth about their daughter, by far the worse part of his job.

Her body was partially nude, just as the others, with her clothes ripped open and hanging to her sides. Her hands, eyes, and mouth were taped and the same message was written across her taped mouth, a sure sign that the same madman had struck again.

As he was joined by other officers and the crime lab, the area surrounding the shed was taped off as they went over every inch of the yard leading to the house as well as into the woods. Behind the shed just inside the woods they found a pair of canvas camouflaged military boots similar to those worn in the Vietnam war, hidden just below the leaves on the ground.

"Send these to the crime lab immediately along with an imprint of the partial tracks leading out of the woods and up to the shed."

As the other investigators completed their work and the coroner arrived to retrieve the body, he walked to the coach's front door rapping and ringing the doorbell, but received no answer.

"Burton, you and Wiley finish up here, I'm heading back over to her parents house and let them know what happened, okay?"

"Sure lieutenant, we'll finish up here and see you back at the precinct later," answered Inspector Burton.

His walk was slow as he rehearsed the words in his mind. You would think he would have the whole explanation down pat by now after four murders and the excruciating task of telling those parents, but it never got easy. What words can you express as you tell parents their daughter is dead, murdered unmercifully at the hands of a killer?

Telling Jack and Hilary Hampton would be no different than telling the others as they both collapsed in each other's arms in disbelief. Stephanie and Randy joined them in their grieving hug as tears flowed endlessly to the sounds of *no, no, not Megan.*

He would stay with them for over an hour explaining what they had found and what would happen next. The questions were always the same, filled with doubt and wonder as to who could have committed such an act, and the answers were always empty and apologetic, simply because he had no answers.

He always felt like he was to blame. What else could he think, he had no answers, very few clues, no real suspects, yet the crimes went on and on. But each crime did give him a little more to go on, a few more little clues that he could piece together, and this murder was no different.

He went on back to the precinct and found Inspectors Burton and Wiley adding the most recent clues to the chalkboard.

"Okay Tom, George, what do we have here?" he asked as he unknotted his tie and threw it over in the direction of his desk.

"Well, in addition to all the same elements as in the previous murders, we have partial footprints, the pair of boots found at the edge of the woods behind the shed, her panties are missing just as Margy McNichol's were, and above all, we have the body in Coach Bannister's shed."

"Okay Tom. Now have we been able to find the coach yet?"

"No Will, as you know he wasn't at home, and George and I went over to the school and he wasn't there either, they hadn't seen him since practice was over."

"Okay, well let's get an APB out for this guy and get him in here today before the sun goes down. I don't want to give him time to think of any excuses or alibis; I want to get his ass at this table and pound him with so many questions he can't think straight."

20

Another two hours would go by before Lieutenant Franklin's wish would come true. The door to the squad room burst open and in walked two officers escorting the handcuffed coach between them.

"Got a present for you lieutenant," snapped one of the officers. "We got him walking back up the jogging path from the school and heading into his back yard."

"Fine, we'll take him," said Lieutenant Franklin as he grabbed the coach by the elbow and led him into the interrogation room.

The other two inspectors followed as the four of them sat down surrounding the table.

Lieutenant Franklin walked over to the water cooler, poured a cup of water and sat it on the table in front of the coach. He poured himself one and sat it on the table in front of his chair as he reached over and unlocked the handcuffs that were restraining

Coach Bannister and sat down taking a small sip of his water.

"What's this all about lieutenant?" asked the coach as he rubbed both of his wrists that were imprinted with the handcuff rings.

"Mr. Bannister, you have a lot of explaining to do, and we are prepared to sit here for as long as it takes to listen to your explanation. So, let's start by you telling us about Megan Hampton."

"What about Megan...she's a great girl who is on my cheerleading squad. In fact, her sister Stephanie was out at school today with her boyfriend Randy, to pick Megan up after practice, but I told her that Megan hadn't shown up for school." There was a slight pause. "Oh my god, did something happen to Megan? Is that why we're here?"

"Yes Mr. Bannister, we found Megan murdered."

There was an immediate silence in the room as the coach put both of his hands over his face and sobbed in disbelief.

"My god, not another one of our girls. What kind of maniac is out there killing all of our girls like this?"

The coach pulled his hands from his face and looked around the room at the three inspectors.

"Please tell me you don't suspect me of these killings."

"Well Mr. Bannister, that's what we're all here for. There seems to be a lot of evidence pointing in your direction on this case, and we would like to give you the benefit of the doubt and hear what you have to say in the way of explanation."

"I'm more than willing to help in any way I can lieutenant. Like I've said so many times, I know all of these girls from the high school. I have coached each and every one of them on the cheerleading squad and know most of their families personally."

"Explain to us your relationship with Megan Hampton."

"Like I said, Megan was on our cheerleading squad last year and this year and one of our most athletic girls. She's extremely popular with all the kids and a real joy to coach."

"You do seem to get very close with all of your cheerleading girls don't you?"

"Now wait a minute lieutenant, yes I do have my own style of coaching and I'll admit I do get very close to the girls, but I am their coach and they are my students, there's a line that is always drawn."

"But I've sat in the stands on many a day and watched all the girls gather around you and you seem to enjoy how these young girls fuss and flirt with you. Now isn't that true?"

"I'll admit I do take advantage of my popularity with the girls, but it seems to energize them into peak performance, they want to perform well for me and yes I do use that to my advantage...but like I said, I have always drawn a line between coach and student."

"And that line was drawn with Megan Hampton too?"

There was a slight pause in his answer that all three of the inspectors picked up on.

"Yes, of course. Megan too."

"Coach, has Megan Hampton ever been inside your home?"

This time there was a longer pause as the coach again buried his face in his hands while shaking his head back and forth. He was still silent.

"Coach, now is the time to tell us the truth. Now is the time to get everything out in the open and be honest with us and don't get yourself deep in a pack of lies. We have already obtained a search warrant and been through your house from top to bottom, so be honest with us coach."

The coach continued to shake his head as he slowly pulled his head up and began wiping the tears from his eyes. He paused another moment to gain his composure.

"I swear to the three of you that I have never done this before in my entire life. I have been a high school coach for over eight years now and my girls and I have always been close. I can't help it, it's just the way I am and the girls just seem to love being around me, but like I said I always draw the line, I have always drawn the line before."

He again paused.

"But Megan was so different. She was just a sweetheart of a girl and just always seemed to want my attention and cuddle up to me, more so than the others. Anyway, a couple of weeks ago she was outside of school after practice when I had finished up in my office and was heading home for the day. I always walk to and from school since it's obviously so close and once in a while some of the girls will walk with me. Anyway, on this particular day Megan was the only one that walked with me."

"And that's up the jogging path through the woods, right?"

"Yes. Well it was an extremely hot day and we had practiced straight through the heat and everyone was hot and exhausted. So when we got to my street she asked if she could possibly have a drink of water before continuing on up the road to home. Well I said sure, no problem and as I went into the house to get her a drink she followed me inside. Well, god, I don't know how it happened but she started looking at me with those big blue eyes and as she handed the empty glass back to me she leaned over and kissed me on the lips. I don't know lieutenant; I just responded for some reason and kissed her back. I mean she's just a beautiful girl and I just don't know what got into me, I've never, never done anything like that before with a student."

The room was silent except for his sobbing. The lieutenant waited a few minutes and then started back with the questions.

"And did this progress into something else?"

"No sir...well I mean yes it kind of did. I mean I never went to bed with her or anything like that, but yes she did return to my house a few times and we became quite intimate."

"Like how many times?"

"A few...in fact, every day this past week."

"And what happened this week?"

"God lieutenant I am so sorry, I just can't believe I let this go on like it did, I just lost all of my senses." He again paused shaking his head. "She stopped by my house each morning before school this week and we had breakfast together and before I knew it we were all over each other."

"So define *all over each other* for me."

"We both were on my bed with very little clothes on."

"Did you have sex?"

"No lieutenant, never...our hands were all over each other but we never had sex one time, never."

"Did you want to?"

"Well of course I did lieutenant, she was a beautiful young girl lying naked beside me but at least I had that much sense."

"Did she want to?"

"Yes, very much so. She kept asking me and asking me and rubbing up against me but I said no every time."

"Is that the truth Mr. Bannister or is the truth that you finally did give in and the two of you had wonderful passionate sex together. She was young, she was beautiful, and you had been taunted every day by these young beautiful teenage girls who just wanted to be with you. So you finally gave in to your desires and went for it all. Then, realizing what you had done, you had no choice but to kill her to keep her quiet. You couldn't let her ruin an eight-year career, your reputation as a coach, you had to do something so you did away with her just like the others. Isn't that the truth Mr. Bannister?"

"No, no, that's not the truth," he yelled back as the tears rolled down both sides of his face. "No, I didn't have sex with her and I didn't murder her or anyone else, I couldn't, I love these girls, they are my life."

"Then why Mr. Bannister did we find the body of Megan Hampton inside your shed in the back yard?"

The stunned coach looked up at him with a startled look.

"My shed? You found her body in my shed?"

"Yes we did, and if you didn't put her there then why are your footprints all around the crime scene?"

"But I'm in my back yard all the time, of course my footprints are going to be there, and besides, there must be hundreds of people with athletic shoes just like mine."

"And what makes you think the murderer had on athletic shoes?"

"Well if you're accusing me of this crime then it must be athletic shoes because that's all I own except for one pair of black dress shoes. I live it tennis shoes, that's my life as a coach."

"You don't own a pair of boots?"

He thought for a moment before answering.

"Well yes I do have one pair of old Marine Corp boots from the service. I use them when I go hunting or in the mud, why?"

"Where are they?"

"I keep them out by the back door on the steps. Whenever it rains I get a big washout from the woods and the whole back yard gets muddy, so I usually slip them on when I'm out there."

"Well Mr. Bannister, we believe the murderer was wearing them when he dragged Megan's body into the shed. Were you wearing them when you murdered her?"

The coach again buried his head in his hands crying.

The interview continued on for another three hours as Coach Bannister continued with his story and denied having anything to do with her murder or the murder of any of the girls.

At the conclusion of the three hours Mr. Bannister was booked on suspicion of murder and having sexual activities with a minor.

21

The word of the coach's arrest spread through town like wildfire as everyone, especially at the high school, could not believe the news. Parents were obviously flabbergasted at the thought of their daughters spending so much time with the coach, as many of them bombarded the school administration with accusations of not properly checking his background and not paying close attention to his extra-curricular activities. But the administration insisted his background was clean and his activities were just that of a young teacher that just got too close to his students.

Weeks would go by with the coach in custody as the homicide team revisited each crime scene studying the impending evidence to see if they could further tie the coach into each crime. The monumental problem confronting Coach Bannister's lawyer was the fact that the coach lived alone thereby having no alibi for his whereabouts other than his own word.

The evidence building against the coach seemed to grow each day as a thorough dusting of his house not only turned up Megan's fingerprints everywhere, but two of the glasses in the cabinet had Margy's fingerprints; boot prints found outside the store where Margy was killed was a perfect match to the coach's boots; found inside his shed were rolls and rolls of gray duct tape and two quart bottles of rubbing alcohol. It all seemed to add up against him with the only missing piece to the puzzle being the girl's panties, all still nowhere to be found.

The coach was officially charged with the murders of Margy McNichol and Megan Hampton but was only suspected of killing the other girls since they just couldn't seem to tie in enough evidence to officially charge him except for the similarity of the murders. Even though each girl had been raped, there was no semen found inside of the girls or anywhere around the crime scenes, so accusing him of raping each of the girls was also questionable.

The trial was set for two months down the road and the investigation team felt confident they could uncover something, some kind of information within the community that would tie the coach to the other crimes.

The lieutenant's first chore in his struggle for more evidence was to talk with the girls on the cheerleading squad so he asked that they gather after school in the gymnasium.

He entered by the main hallway, feeling the stifling heat hit him in the face as he swung open the double doors. This gym was no different than any other school gym, with twenty-foot ceilings, chain-link grating covering the windows, wooden bleachers spanning the length of one side, and a colorful wooden painted floor with the patterns of basketball, gymnastics, and volleyball laid out in different colors.

He paused as the doors shut behind him and loosened his necktie in hopes of gaining some relief from the heat of the room.

"Whew, it sure is hot in here," he said as he slowly walked towards the group of girls sitting at the far end of the bleachers. Their chatter stopped as they all glanced his way.

They were a beautiful group of girls, all dressed in their cheerleading uniforms, most of them with their hair pulled back and tied behind their head in a ponytail. He counted nine of them as he approached, pulling up a metal folding chair and sitting down to face them.

"Good afternoon girls and thanks for coming here to meet with me today."

"Good afternoon," they responded in unison as the three rows of them shifted left or right to get a good view of him seated on the gym floor.

"I've asked you here today to talk a little bit about your coach and some of the things that have been happening lately. I would expect each of you to give me honest answers to my questions and if any of you would rather talk to me in private rather than in a group, feel free to let me know afterwards. Now...let's start out with just a general question for all of you, how do you feel about Coach Bannister?"

There was a slight moment of silence as they looked around at each other waiting for someone to voluntarily break the quiet.

"He's the greatest," said a voice from the last row, whose name on her uniform read Mary. "Coach is always there for us and spends so much of his own time working with each one of us to make us the best we can be.

"I agree," said another. "There is no way I can believe he had anything to do with the murders of our friends, he just isn't like that. He's kind and cares about each one of us individually and as a team."

"That's why there's such a waiting list to get on the squad, because everyone likes him so much," another voice added.

He held up the palm of his hand to silence the group.

"Okay, so the general consensus is that Coach Bannister is a great guy and wouldn't harm anyone, especially one of his students. Is that what I'm hearing from all of you?"

They all shook their heads in agreement.

"All right, let's talk about after school activities. Have any of you ever been with the coach after cheerleading practice, say off of school grounds? Raise your hand if you have."

To his amazement they all raised their hand.

"All of you have seen the coach outside of school activities?" he asked.

They each shook their heads in agreement. Looking around he noticed that Mary, the first girl to speak, seemed extremely fidgety and uncomfortable.

"Okay Mary, you spoke first so let's start with you. When have you seen the coach outside of school and why?"

"I think I can speak for all the girls' lieutenant. We have all at one time or another left practice with the coach and walked home with him. Most of us live in the same neighborhoods around school and occasionally walk home instead of riding, so since he lives on the way home, we've all walked with him."

"And you've walked through the woods down the jogging path to his house?"

"Yes sir," she answered as each of them nodded their heads in agreement.

"Did you ever go into his home with him?"

"Well I know I have but only with a group of other girls. He asked us if we wanted something to drink so we all went in his kitchen. That's happened a few times in the last two years."

"Have any of you been in his home alone with him? Raise your hand."

Four of the nine hands went up.

"Okay, you Natalie. What happened when you went in with him?"

Natalie smiled slightly as she brushed her bangs out of her eyes. "Well nothing happened…I mean we were talking the whole way up the path and when we got to his house he asked if I wanted something to drink and I said sure. He asked me in and we got some iced tea and went back out to his porch and sat and talked. That's it."

"That's what happened to me too," answered Paula as she shook her head in agreement. "He just asked me in to get a drink and we sat in his living room and talked about school and cheerleading. The coach is a great guy and a real looker if I do say so myself. I didn't mind spending time with him at all."

They all giggled as a group at her answer.

"Okay girls, listen up. I know the coach is a handsome guy and all of you love being with him but we have a serious matter in front of us and we need to think seriously about this. Now please, be perfectly honest with me on this next question, it could affect someone's life. Has the coach ever touched you inappropriately or asked to?"

Again in unison they all shook their head no.

Mary spoke up again for the group. "Lieutenant we all have an awesome respect for the coach and so do our parents, that's why he's so popular and so well liked. He's just a great coach and a great guy. We wouldn't want anyone else coaching us but him. Right girls?"

They all kind of raised their arms pumping their fists as they agreed.

At that point the lieutenant knew he had an audience of dedicated girls who loved their teacher and would continue to defend him no matter what. He thanked them for their time and asked Mary if she would join him outside for a few minutes.

Mary reminded him so much of his own daughter both in her looks and her personality. She was only a few inches shorter than him, with long auburn curly hair and a bright white smile that lit up the room. Even though she was the first to speak today he couldn't help but notice the feeling of awkwardness she had while discussing the coach and he knew he needed to get her alone to see if maybe she was holding something back.

"Mary is there anything at all you'd like to tell me now that we're alone."

"No sir, why?" she asked.

"Well, to tell you the truth, you seemed a little squirmy to me in the gym when I was asking questions about Coach Bannister. I just thought maybe since we were alone you might have something you'd like to make me aware of."

22

There was a sense of calm that reverberated throughout the community once the coach was booked and the horror of what had taken place settled in.

Fran and Mike continued to talk of moving their wedding forward and getting married when they both finished their second year of college, which was right around the corner. Stephanie and Randy became inseparable once her sister Megan's funeral was over and the two of them leaned heavily on each other to recover from their past tragedies. Rhonda and Billie had also gotten extremely close since Randy's last party and rumor had it that he was about to ask her to marry him, but rumors have a way of being exaggerated so everyone was just waiting for the official announcement.

And then there was Becky and Brad, the secret couple no one knew existed. Brad's entire life and character had come into question with all the suspicions pointing towards him, the stranger in the crowd, the out-of-towner who had taken up with all the college kids. But he had taken the smart route; he laid low and cooperated fully with the police whenever they questioned him. He had nothing to hide but as a businessman in town he needed the people's confidence and trust in order for his business to continue to succeed. Running a successful photography studio nowadays is a challenge with all the digital technology out there for the world to use, so he needed to be adventuresome, creative and have a knockout personality, and Brad's strongpoint is his personality.

Brad's business had finally returned to normalcy since the coach had been booked as all suspicions shifted off of him and people again became confident in his work and his character. Business was so good that Brad approached Mr. Thomas about letting Becky model for him at several shows he was hosting in a few of the surrounding towns. In years past, he travelled to the malls in the area to display his work and take on-the-spot pictures to enlist new business, so this year he had talked Becky into modeling at the shows for him and allowing him to display some of her portfolio shots. She of course agreed immediately since she would be spending time with him, but was fearful that her parents might not be as enthusiastic, so Brad asked if he could speak with them over dinner and they agreed.

Brad arrived at the house about six-thirty in the evening for the planned seven o'clock dinner. Becky greeted him at the door of course and led him into the den where the rest of the family was sitting, except for her mom who was in the adjoining kitchen preparing dinner.

"Good to see you Mr. Thomas," Brad said as he extended his hand.

"Good to see you too Brad, have a seat."

Brad greeted both Fran and her mom before sitting down then purposely went over to the large single seat so as not to be too close to Becky. He looked over at her as he sat down watching her playfully pucker her bottom lip in disappointment.

"We're certainly glad to see you cleared of all those ridiculous charges Brad as I'm sure you are too."

"To say the least Mr. Thomas; it's really a tough situation to be in and one I hope I'm never faced with again. I mean, I live alone and spend most of my time in the shop or upstairs in my apartment alone, so not having an alibi for so many of the times they asked me about was frustrating but I didn't know what else to say. I was faced with these accusations being thrown at me and really had no defense at all. It was completely scary. I kept thinking about all the men in prison who continually plead their innocence but have no way to prove or disprove it and here I was about to be in that same situation. I was scared to death."

"Well we were scared for you Brad," said Mrs. Thomas from the kitchen. The two rooms were in fact one, just separated by a kitchen counter with stools.

"Well I really want to thank everyone who stood by me and believed in me during the whole ordeal. I mean I'm still scared about the whole thing because the guy has never been caught and he obviously tried to tie me in to the whole thing by planting that bag in my shop and stealing one of my cigarette stubs. Who's to say he couldn't do it again and I'm right back in jail again."

"Everyone believes in you Brad and we're all ready to stand behind you when you need us," said Fran.

"Well thanks to all of you. You all are the closest thing to family that I have since I moved here so I really do appreciate you trust."

"And we love you like a brother," said Becky as she laughed out loud.

"Well I think of you as like a little sister to me too," Brad said immediately to try and cover up her laughter.

"Okay dinner's ready ya'll. Fran, if you and Becky can help me carry this stuff to the table we'll be ready to eat."

They all proceeded to the table with Becky leading Brad to the chair right beside hers. After some idle chit-chat over dinner Brad decided to bring up his reason for visiting.

"Mr. and Mrs. Thomas, the reason I asked to come over tonight was to ask you both a question."

Becky began squirming in her chair and tapping her fork as Brad continued his talk.

"As you know this entire ordeal has been tough on me and very tough on my business. People stopped coming into the shop even though I was released and I seemed to lose the respect of everyone, except your daughter who never stopped believing in me. Becky's a wonderful girl and I have I have the utmost respect for her and appreciate all the time she has spent with me to further my photography business."

At this point Mrs. Thomas started to squirm in her chair a little bit fearing the direction the conversation was headed.

"Recently though my business had picked up considerably and I believe that is because of the arresting of Coach Bannister which has taken the heat off of me. But thanks to Becky and the rest of our crowd, they have led everyone back to my shop and I think people are believing in me again as they did before."

"Well I think it was only human nature Brad for people of this town to be scared of you since you are so new to the town and with all the suspicions pointing in your direction. You know most people in this town don't really know you the way we do and the way the other families of the kids do. They only see this young man who lives alone and hangs around with a crowd of kids younger than him who is suddenly arrested for suspicion of murder, so naturally the community shuns you. It's only natural."

"Oh I know and I don't blame them one bit. But my point is that my business suffered immensely and it took quite a while to get that trust back from the community. Anyway, what I'm leading to is that I have decided to expand my business a little and try and pull in business from some of the surrounding communities within a short distance from here. I've always just been satisfied with local business, but my goals have always been much higher and I believe the time is right for me to do a little expanding. So what I've done is booked some photography shows in a couple of the malls in the surrounding area, right now one at Chatham Mall in Lancaster and one in Chase Mall in Lexington. The shows will be on weekends, all day Saturday and Sunday, and I'll be set up in the center court displaying my pictures and offering free portraits."

"Sounds like a great business opportunity to me," remarked Mr. Thomas. "I think it sounds like a perfect time to try it and show everyone else how talented you are and what you have to offer."

"Yes sir and thank you for the compliment," Brad answered as he looked over at Becky who was grinning from ear to ear.

"So...what I wanted to ask was if I could have your permission to take Becky along with me to my shows. She is a perfect model and I think it would be super beneficial for me to have an experienced model with me to compliment my display. A lot of the pictures I will be displaying are of Becky anyway so I would like her to be there, and besides, if I get busy I could really use the help and she probably knows my business more than anyone around."

There was a moment of silence as Mr. and Mrs. Thomas looked each other's way waiting for the other to speak.

"Well Brad, I'm not sure what to say at the moment."

"Oh Dad say yes, please," Becky pleaded. "I would just love to go with him and it would give me some work experience for modeling as well as hopefully some sales experience. Please."

"What do you think mom," Mr. Thomas said as her looked over at his wife.

"I think maybe it's something we should think about Bob," she answered as she looked over at Becky's jubilant face. Knowing how Becky felt about Brad made it difficult for her to be anything but hesitant.

"Well I certainly sense the hesitation that both of you have but I hope you understand that I'll take very good care of her and never let her out of my sight the whole weekend."

"Are you planning on staying overnight up there?" Mr. Thomas asked.

"Well yes I was planning on it but I certainly would be getting Becky a separate room."

Brad watched as her parents stared at each other with doubtful looks.

"I can tell you're not comfortable with that by the way you're looking at each other. I tell you what, if I may suggest something else. The first mall is just thirty-five miles up the road so I'd certainly be willing to wrap things up Saturday night and bring Becky home for the night then pick her back up Sunday morning. It means that much to me to have her there for this event if that will make your decision easier."

"Please mom and dad...it could mean a lot for my career future."

"If it would help the situation I would be willing to go along with Becky that weekend just as kind of a big sister," volunteered Fran.

"There, that's perfect," snapped Becky, "Fran will be right there with me all the time. What do you say; please...just give it a try."

"Well, if that's the case, if it's okay with your father it's okay with me."

All eyes were on her dad as the whole table waited for a response.

"Oh all right. We'll try it once and see how it goes."

Both girls cheered and Brad thanked everyone for being there for him.

"But I will say this Brad, I expect you to be there at every moment and watch over my daughters completely. I don't want them alone for one second in that mall or during the trip. If that is understood then you have our permission for this first show."

Brad was elated but wondered how he would control Becky as she rubbed his leg with her foot underneath the table.

23

To say the least, Brad was ecstatic with the decision and you can imagine how thrilled Becky was. The first mall show was in three weeks so Brad had plenty of time to get all the plans in place for the show that he hoped would catapult him into a new spotlight of expanding his business venture even further. Becky of course couldn't thank her sister enough for volunteering her time to the weekend as she was convinced that was the sole reason her parents decided to let her go. She wasn't sure how Brad felt but she knew that if that weekend went well it could mean that she could accompany him on other trips without her sister, or so she hoped.

The bad part of the whole thing was that Brad would have to spend a lot of the week out of town making all the arrangements at the mall for the show, so Becky used her lonely time by catching up on her studies to be sure she kept her grades up. The last thing she wanted was to have all the plans cast aside because her grades were slipping.

The three murder cases seemed to take a backseat in the community as everyone waited for the preliminary trial to start. The community and school system were devastated with all the evidence piled up against the coach, but seemed convinced that the police had their man. The cheerleading practices were put on hold since no interim coach had been appointed by the school system, but the girls, who were ever faithful to Coach Bannister, practiced on their own each day with the help of a few of the old cheerleaders, namely Rhonda Collins and Stephanie Hampton. They also believed in the coach and were happy to show their support for his innocence by helping out his girls while he wasn't there.

Lieutenant Franklin dropped in on the cheerleading practice every once in a while and on this day found Randy in the stands as well as Fran Thomas and her dad along with Brad Townsend.

"Good afternoon folks," snapped the lieutenant as he walked up the bleachers to where most of them were gathered.

"Hey Lieutenant, good to see you again. What brings you down to the school this afternoon?" questioned Mr. Thomas.

"Oh I just like dropping by every now and again to see how the girls are doing. I might ask the same of all of you. What brings you here this afternoon?"

"Same thing," answered Mr. Thomas. "Fran and I dropped by to watch some of her old friends on the squad, namely Stephanie and Rhonda who are helping out the girls in the coach's absence."

"I'm here to watch my girl Stephanie work it out," laughed Randy.

"Good to see you again Randy. I'm glad things are working out for you," the lieutenant responded with a laugh. "How about you Brad?"

"Oh I'm visiting with Fran and her dad while we wait for Becky to get here from the library.

"Great," Lieutenant Franklin replied as he sat down to watch the practice. "How's business been Brad?"

"Pretty good lieutenant. I'm trying to expand out to a few of the other communities by doing some shows at a few of the malls. Things look real promising thanks to Mr. and Mrs. Thomas' permission to let Becky model for me at the shows. I can't thank them enough for that."

"You're quite welcome Brad," said Mr. Thomas. "I just hope this venture helps you in your business as well as Becky in her modeling career."

"Well good, I hope everything works out for everyone," the lieutenant replied as he swung around to watch the cheerleaders.

Only a few minutes passed by before they all heard a toot of the horn and turned towards the parking lot.

"Well there's your mom and Becky coming to get us for dinner I suspect," said Mr. Thomas to Fran.

"Aren't you coming over for dinner tonight Brad?" asked Fran.

"Yes that's at six-thirty right?"

"Right, do you want to ride over with us?"

"No I have to stop by the studio and tie up a few loose ends but I promise I'll be on time. I wouldn't miss a home cooked meal for anything," Brad answered as he too got up and headed for his car.

"Okay, Fran tell your mom I'll be home by dinnertime. I have to slip by the bank on the way home to pick up some paperwork that has to be mailed tonight. I left it on my desk by mistake."

"Okay Dad. See you at dinner, and you too Brad," said Fran as she jumped down off the bleachers and headed towards the waiting car. "See you later Lieutenant. You too Randy."

Practice on the field was breaking up as most of the girls headed for the locker rooms to change except for Stephanie who ran up on the bleachers to sit beside Randy.

Lieutenant Franklin and Brad said their goodbyes as they too jumped off the bleachers and headed for their cars in the parking lot.

As the lieutenant drove away he couldn't help but feel relieved that he had found his murderer and the community was getting back to normal. The evidence that he had accumulated against the coach seemed overwhelming and he firmly believed the murder spree was over.

Or was it?

24

The Lieutenant had barely made it home that evening when the phone rang. It was Jack and Cindy Collins informing him that Rhonda was due home from cheerleading practice over four hours ago and they were worried sick.

"We're sorry to bother you at home Lieutenant, but when Rhonda didn't show up at the house and none of her friends that we called had seen her since practice, we became worried. We grabbed your card that you had given us at the community meeting and called right away. Can you help us, please."

He arrived at the Collins' house within minutes and sat down with them to hear all the details of Rhonda's day.

"I was at that practice today," the lieutenant informed them. "I stopped by on my way past the school and sat in the stands talking to Randy, Fran Thomas and her father, and Brad Townsend. We were all watching Rhonda and Stephanie Hampton work out routines with the squad of girls. When it was over and we all left the bleachers, Randy and Stephanie were sitting there talking and the rest of the girls had headed into the school locker rooms to change."

"Including Rhonda?" asked Jack Collins.

"Well I assume so," the lieutenant answered while looking into the air thinking. "You know I can't say for sure that I saw her heading into the school specifically, it was just a large group of girls and I assumed she was in that group. I know for a fact that she was on the field along with Stephanie leading them, but I just can't say that she was in that group heading for the school lockers. But I know someone who will and that's Stephanie Hampton. I'll call her right now."

He proceeded to take his cell phone out of his coat pocket and dialed her number.

"Stephanie, this is Lieutenant Franklin with a question for you. Today at cheerleading practice I saw you and Rhonda leading the high school girls through some cheers. When that was over I saw you go up in the stands with Randy and was wondering if you knew where Rhonda went?"

Jack and Cindy Collins hung on the edge of their seat as they watched him pause for the answers.

"Okay, and did you and Randy stay in the bleachers for a while or did you leave right after me?"

Another pause.

"Okay, and you didn't meet up with Rhonda again, you just left with Randy?"

"Okay thanks Stephanie."

"No we hope nothing is wrong, we're just trying to track Rhonda down and she hasn't come home yet. Okay, goodbye."

He clicked off of the call and put his phone away.

"No, she said her and Randy stayed for just a few minutes and then left in his car and went over to her house so she could change. He was still there at her house staying for dinner. She said the last she saw of Rhonda was when she went into the locker rooms with the rest of the girls to change. That's it."

"So what do we do now Lieutenant?" they asked as he could see tears beginning to run down the side of her face. "We're scared to death that something awful has happened to her. She's always on time and when she isn't she always calls us. Always!"

"Now try not to get too upset, we'll find her. It's only been a couple of hours but I'll put a call out to all patrol cars to keep their eyes open for her and in the mean time why don't you two think of any other friends she may have stopped to talk with and give them a call. I'm going to ride over to the school and trace her steps to see if I can find anything. Stay here and I'll give you a call or stop back by."

They agreed and with that Lieutenant Franklin left the house and drove over to the school parking lot. There was no one around at this hour so he parked his car on the lot and decided to walk the path through the woods to the coach's house and back to see if he saw any trace of Rhonda.

As he walked he scanned continually from left to right combing the wooded brush for any telltale sign that a struggle or attack had occurred. About half way into the woods he was confronted by a bicycle rider who slowed down to pass him. He stopped the young man, whom he didn't know, and asked if he had seen anyone in or around the woods during his trip but the reply was no.

He reached the coach's house and randomly walked around the house, the yard, and the shed out back to make sure there were no signs of Rhonda and in fact there was nothing. The yellow investigation tape was still up and blowing in the wind as it surrounded the shed where the last crime had taken place. Since all the investigation had been completed he gathered up the yellow tape and threw it in a trash can at the back of the coach's driveway.

He paused for a minute after putting the lid back on the can listening for what he thought was a faint murmur or sound. He walked around the house again listening intently but decided it must have been a noise from the woods and left to walk the pathway back to the school.

This time he passed two teenage boys jogging together and again stopped them and asked the same questions. He also asked if they knew Rhonda Collins and they both said no that they didn't go to this school but the high school on the other side of town.

He reached his car and sat in the front seat just scanning the area surrounding the parking lot and practice fields hoping he would see her and a friend casually strolling without a care in the world. He thought about his daughter and how much pain and frustration he would be going through if she were missing like Rhonda. It was truly a parents' nightmare that no one deserves to go through but unfortunately a few of the families in his town have had to.

He felt relieved for himself that it wasn't his daughter, but guilty that he couldn't have done more for the other grieving families that he felt he had failed.

25

Her breathing became more and more labored as she laid on the cold floor trying desperately to free her hands. It was exhausting trying to breathe just through her nose and the tiny opening in the tape while still struggling to move her body in a position that she could use all her strength to pull the tape loose.

Rhonda Collins was still alive!

She relaxed her body to try and calm herself down and catch her breath as her cold naked body shivered in the cold house. She had been in the coach's house several times and knew where his telephone was but just couldn't manage to muster the strength to roll over and get to her feet to reach it and didn't know if she could find it with tape over her eyes. She sensed she was still in the living room but wasn't sure.

She was tired. She had been struggling for over four hours now and breathing through her nose just didn't seem to get her enough air. Her breathing was so fast that she continually became dizzy from the lack of oxygen and the smell of alcohol was so strong it burned her nostrils with every breath. The tiny opening she created in the tape across her mouth was the only help she had and she didn't want to do anything that would seal that air hole up again. Each struggling effort made her head spin from lightheadedness as she continued to suck in air through her nose, so much work, too little air.

She made the only sound she could, a muffled hum, when she heard the noises outside the house but if only she had thought to kick her feet on the floor.

Her mind continually raced at full speed as she replayed the events since she left practice and headed home walking down the path through the woods. She had walked that path a thousand times since she started school at Forest Hill High and never feared anything would happen even though Margy had been killed there. She just felt that was an oddball occurrence and didn't think twice about using the path again to go home every day. And anyway, the suspected culprit was in jail even though she agreed with the other girls that the coach couldn't have done it. And now she knew he didn't do it because he was in jail and she still had been attacked.

She shivered involuntarily as her bare body was so cold in the nighttime air and she still felt the pain of the forcible attack on her. He was so gentle with her at the beginning of the rape but as it went on his excitement caused him to go deeper and deeper inside of her causing her unbearable pain.

She tried for the hundredth time to hold her breath and blow out of the tiny hole to enlarge it but the tape was just too strong against her mouth. It took all the energy she had and her body went limp from exhaustion. She lay motionless as she had done when her attacker pressed his hand against her mouth and nose to suffocate her. She knew she was going to pass out any second so she let her body fall motionless and he let up thinking she was gone.

But now she was just so tired and exhausted from the constant struggling. She just needed someone to find her.

The lieutenant pulled his car into the Collins driveway, turned the engine off and just sat there staring out of the windshield. He knew there was something that bothered him but he just wasn't sure what it was. His mind kept running through this evening and where he had gone and the nagging feeling that he was leaving something out. He knew after all these years as a detective that his natural instinct was what helped him solve so many of his cases. Yet he just couldn't put a finger on what bothered him at this moment.

He was pulled out of his blank stare by a rapping on the car window.

"Is everything okay lieutenant?" questioned both the parents as they stared intently through the closed car window.

"No I'm sorry I didn't find anything at the school and talked to a few people in the area but no one saw anything of Rhonda. Did either of you have any luck contacting her friends?"

"No, no luck. None of the girls she was with today have seen her since she left the school to walk home."

"So she definitely was supposed to walk home from cheerleading today?"

"Yes," answered her mom. "She always walks home from helping the girls at cheerleading the same way she always walked home when she went to school there and had cheerleading practice herself."

"We stopped her from walking home alone while all those killings were going on, but now that he's been caught we just told her to go back to life as normal," said her dad.

"That's still not a wise decision Mr. Collins. We have Coach Bannister jailed as a primary suspect but we haven't to this point proven anything. Why don't the two of you just go into the house and wait for me to give you a call, I've still got a few things I want to investigate. If you hear anything call my cell phone right away."

They agreed as they walked back into the house hand in hand trying to comfort the fear they both were experiencing.

He slowly pulled his car out of the driveway and over to the curb. His blank stare resurfaced as he tried to figure out what was eating at him. He played back in his mind his trip to the school and the three people he had talked to on the path in the woods but he just knew none of them were probably suspects in this disappearance; they were just normal people going through their daily routine.

He thought if he drove back over to the school parking lot maybe something would click in his mind, but when he arrived and parked the car he again just sat puzzled by this nagging feeling.

He sat retracing his steps and that's when it hit him, the sound he heard when he was looking around

Coach Bannister's house. That must be what is bothering him.

He started the car back up and drove all the way around the woods to the coach's street and parked the car in his driveway. Once he got out and slammed the door shut he gingerly walked towards the back of the house where he first heard the noise that seemed to be imbedded in his mind.

Rhonda rolled ever so slightly to her side and held her breath as she listened for what sounded like a car door shutting nearby. If she heard someone she would do everything she could this time to alert the visitor.

But what if it's her attacker who has come back to get something or attack her again? My God what does she do now? Should she possibly risk her life by letting her attacker know she is still alive, or keep quiet and chance that this intruder could save her from this horrid situation?

She lay motionless as her mind raced with indecision as her breathing got more labored and more intense.

Outside she heard footsteps coming off the driveway and onto the back porch steps. Tears were filling the tape around her closed eyes as fear again entered her cold scared body. She didn't want to get raped again and she certainly didn't want to die. The footsteps traveled up the steps and onto the porch as her heart pounded with fear.

"Hello, this is Lieutenant Tim Franklin of the police department, is anyone there?"

A sign of relief exited Rhonda's nose as she heard the voice of a friend and not a foe.

She began to flail her body repeatedly kicking the floor and trying to project as much sound from her inner voice as she could. Her feet pounded and pounded the floor in desperation. She had to make him hear her, this was her chance at survival.

Lieutenant Franklin's rushed to the door as he heard a repeat of the sound that had bothered him. He heard the whimpering grow louder followed by a continuous banging. He drew his service revolver and threw the door open pointing his weapon straight ahead as he entered the dark house. He knelt down near the floor with his gun pointed straight ahead as he reached up and flicked on the light.

There straight ahead lying on the floor was Rhonda's naked body with her legs and feet moving up and down to make as much noise as she could with her tied aching body.

He rushed over to her side and pulled the tape off of her mouth in one swift hard yank.

"Rhonda, are you alone or is someone else here?" he questioned as his eyes never left the dimly lit surrounding room.

"I'm alone," she said as she burst out in a relieved but weak cry.

He slowly pulled the tape off of her eyes and rolled her over on her side to also get the tape from around her two wrists thereby releasing her hands. She immediately threw her arms around his neck crying now as loudly as she could. He picked her up and carried her into the nearest bedroom flicking on the light as they walked in. Laying her on the bed he pulled the covers over her naked body to get her warm and comfortable as he pulled out his cell phone and called for an ambulance and detectives.

"Rhonda are you okay?" he asked as he pulled a handkerchief from his pocket and brushed her tears aside. "Are you hurt in any way?"

"He raped me, he raped me twice," she managed to say as her voice quivered with fear.

Her body was shaking uncontrollably as he wrapped the covers more around her and pulled her close to him while rubbing her back to comfort her in any way he could.

"You're safe now Rhonda, I promise no one will hurt you anymore. I promise sweetie!"

Within minutes he could hear the sound of the ambulance pulling in front of the house and before long the house was a scurry of activity.

He immediately called Rhonda's parents and told them he had found her and they should meet her at Harford Memorial Hospital.

As the medics were wheeling her out of the house she asked for the lieutenant and as he bent down to hear her whispers she said *thank you for saving my life*. She took his hand and opening hers, she put a shirt button in his palm.

"I tore this off his sleeve," she whispered.

This time a tear came to his eye.

Once she was loaded into the ambulance they began their investigation of the crime scene. He would wait a few hours before going to the hospital to meet with her and see if she could give him any clues as to the perpetrator.

This was the first girl to survive one of the brutal attacks that has devastated this community, so he was hoping beyond all hope that she saw something or if fact knew who her attacker was.

26

She looked much better when he entered the private room, calmer, less pale and breathing normal.

"Hello again Miss Rhonda," he said as both parents stood up and approached him, Jack with his hand extended and Cindy grabbing him to give him a hug.

"Lieutenant you know we can't thank you enough for finding our daughter," Jack Collins said.

"You literally saved her life," cried her mother Cindy. "If it wasn't for you Rhonda would still be lying on that cold floor tied up and struggling to survive. You are truly a hero."

"I'm the one who really wants to give you a hug," said Rhonda from her bed.

He walked over to the bed and bent down as both her arms wrapped tightly around his neck. She hugged and hugged as he held her close and imagined how he would be feeling if this was his daughter who had been so brutally attacked and left for dead.

"How did you ever find me?" she asked.

"It was total instinct," he answered as he sat gingerly on the edge of the bed. "You can ask your parents. When I was at their house earlier I just had something nagging at me that I just couldn't figure out until I got back at the school. When I came earlier and walked the path to the coach's house I just heard a slight sound that was totally out of the ordinary for the area. It should have bothered me more then but I just chalked it off as a sound from the woods because it came and went so quickly. And when I came back that second time I knew I had to investigate that small telltale sound. And luckily it was you."

"I was so frustrated with myself because I didn't make more noise when I heard you outside the first time, but I was just so tired of struggling to get free that I was worn out, and then you were gone," Rhonda said as she settled back into the pillow.

She looked so different lying on the pillow with her long auburn hair cascading down her shoulders; a far cry from the snarled up mess that she looked when he discovered her body.

"You look wonderful now Rhonda, I hope they're treating you good here," he said as he reached over and squeezed her hand. "Do you feel like talking business for a minute?"

"Sure."

"Can you tell me what happened?"

"Sure. I wrapped up cheerleading practice and went into the locker room with the rest of the girls. Stephanie and I have been helping coach the girls while the coach is locked up."

"I know, go on."

"Well Stephanie went up to the bleachers to talk with Randy so I went in with the rest of the girls and cleaned up and changed. When I came out her and Randy had just pulled out of the parking lot so I headed down towards the woods to pick up the path for home. I always walk that way home, have for years and years."

"Always alone?" the lieutenant asked.

"Most of the time yes but I've also walked it with other girls and even the coach on several occasions. It leads right to his house so that's the way he goes home too. It just depended on the time of day whether I was alone or not. Anyway, I was alone today and headed home as I always have, just me and my gym bag. I was making the last turn, right where it curves around to see the coach's house straight ahead. It was then that I heard the snap of a branch and before I could turn around he tackled me to the ground."

"You hadn't seen anyone around to this point?"

"No, and if you know that area, right at the small bend in the path, you know there are a lot of tall fat bushes that almost hide the woods. I guess that's where he was hiding, right behind those bushes. It's so funny because every time I walk that path, for all of these years, when I get to those bushes I always go to the other side of the path away from them just thinking that it's the perfect place for someone to hide."

"Did you get to see him at all?" asked the lieutenant, hoping he would get a positive answer.

"No," she answered as a tear started to glide down her cheek for the first time. "He just came out of nowhere. Before I could even react he tackled me to the ground and my face was in the dirt. Right away he was on top of me and I couldn't move he was so heavy.

I tried to turn my head to look at him and at that instant he had a piece of tape slapped over my eyes and within seconds another piece over my mouth. I swear he must have had that tape cut and ready because it was instantaneous. From that point on I was in total darkness. But I do remember one thing, I remember just before he put the tape over my eyes I remember seeing blue."

"The color blue?"

"Yes blue, I think it was his shirt sleeve. I know he had on a long sleeve shirt and the color must have been light blue."

"So what happened next, did he lead you into the house?"

"Yes he pulled me up by my arm and led me up the steps and into the coach's house. I started kicking at him once we got into the house but he immediately forced me to the floor and taped my ankles together so I couldn't kick him anymore."

"Did he talk to you?"

"Not up to that point. He did grunt a little when I kicked him twice but no words."

"Go on."

At this point the tears really stated forming in her eyes and her body began to tremble.

"Lieutenant, do we need to do this now?" asked her father.

"No it's okay Dad, I can do this," Rhonda said as she reached up and wiped her tears aside. Taking a huge breath of air to continue.

"Mr. and Mrs. Collins, maybe it's best that you not listen to these details of your daughters struggle, it will only make your pain that much more intense. Why don't you wait outside in the hallway until we're finished?" the lieutenant said in a sorrowful plea.

"Okay, I think you're right...let's wait outside dear," he said to his wife as he led her out of the room. "If this becomes too much for you sweetie you just let the lieutenant know that you've had enough. Okay Rhonda?"

"Okay Dad," she said with a slight smile of confidence for him.

Once they left the room and the door closed she continued her story.

"I could feel him kneel down beside me and he was whispering something but to be honest my breathing was so hard and my heart was pounding so strong that I just couldn't hear what he was saying at all. I finally held my breath a little bit and heard him say *beautiful, absolutely beautiful.* At that point he started unbuttoning my blouse and slowly taking all my clothes off. Oh lieutenant I was so scared and so thoroughly humiliated, I was just dying."

"I can only imagine Rhonda. I have two daughters and I know how devastated they both would be to even think about being in that situation, or any girl for that matter. Can you continue?"

"Yes. Once he got all my clothes off he just started touching and playing with me. He fondled and played with my breasts for the longest time and then ended up licking them and putting them in his mouth."

At this point she hesitated to catch her breath and again wipe the tears from her face.

"Take your time Rhonda, I know this is painful to remember."

"Next he took the tape from around my ankles and began to spread my legs open. I immediately tried to keep them tight together by crossing my ankles, then once he separated them I began to try and kick him again. At this point he leaned over to my ear and whispered *we can do this gently or we can do this real rough, it's up to you,* I'll never forget those words. So I relaxed and figured it was going to happen and if I cooperated maybe he would just do it and leave. I let him spread my legs open and he again began to play with me down there. I could tell he was getting real excited because his breathing was getting heavier and heavier. He finally got up and I could hear his belt buckle hit the floor as his pants dropped. He got on top of me and forced my legs to open real wide and I could feel him go inside of me. It hurt so very much but I just wanted it to be over so I tried to control my fear and pain as much as I could. Amazingly it was over quickly as I heard him breathe a sigh of relief and then he was out of me. I figured it was finally over and I laid there wondering what was next. Was he going to kill me or just leave? It was so quiet for the longest time; I just didn't hear anything but his breathing. After what seemed like forever my biggest fear came back as he again began playing with me all over. At this point he was really gentle and seemed to stop every so often, I sensed that he was pulling back just looking at me because he would open my legs and pull my knees up so my feet were flat on the ground and just keep pushing my knees further and further apart until I couldn't stand it. All the time he just kept muttering *beautiful, simply beautiful, I'm finally doing what you want.* He got on top of me again and this time took forever to finish. It was just so horrible and it hurt so very much."

She began to really cry at this point and the lieutenant stopped the conversation to let her regain her composure, but she insisted on continuing to get the whole story out and finished.

She continued.

"At this point he seemed to be getting himself together and cleaning up or something. I could hear him like rubbing things and moving across the floor, so I assume he was wiping up his evidence. Next he started cleaning me up. He wiped my entire body down with this smelly alcohol solution that made me gag the smell was so strong. He wiped every inch of me twice and it stung so bad when he wiped in between my legs, but I sensed he enjoyed every minute of it as he continued to say those same words again and again. I guess that's why he did that while I was still alive because he wanted to enjoy watching me move and jiggle. Gross huh?"

"No sick is a better word Rhonda."

"I think in my mind I was still hoping that since I hadn't seen who he was that he would just go and leave me. But I thought of the other girls who had been murdered earlier this year and just knew I would be next. Funny, I never believed the coach was guilty of those crimes but now I was lying there hoping it *was* the coach and that this was just a copycat rapist who would get his pleasures and then leave me. Anyway, he knelt down beside me and whispered in my ear *'you are so very beautiful and I have watched you for a long time and wanted you so much. It was definitely worth the wait, you were wonderful in bed and absolutely beautiful to look at. I'm so glad you wanted me to do this. Thank you Rhonda and goodnight'*. My heart skipped a beat and my breathing was so hard that's all you could hear in the room. I think it really startled him. He pinched my nose shut but not before I took the longest breath I have ever taken in my life. I think my experience from being on the high school swim team for all those years really paid off because I knew I could hold my breath for over a minute. So he pinched my nose shut and I waited a few seconds and just let my body go limp as if I weren't breathing any longer. Within seconds he let my nose go and I sensed him just looking at me and then I could hear him gathering up some things and he was gone. He wasn't out the door a half a second before I slowly let out a breath and quietly listened. I didn't hear a car start or any doors shut immediately, but I heard his footsteps walking away and then the sound in the distance of a car starting, so I assumed he parked a little ways down the road."

She again wiped her tears and took a deep breath.

"Rhonda I want to thank you for that detailed story. I know it was hard but I think you know how necessary it was," said the lieutenant as he again reached over and squeezed her hand in appreciation.

"So at what point did you pull off the button you gave me?" he asked.

"When we first went into the house and began to kick and struggle with him, my hand slid down his arm and I tugged at his shirtsleeve and pulled the button off. I don't think he really knew it because of the struggle and because I just kept it clinched in my hand from that moment on."

"Well hopefully that will help us get this guy. Its little clues like that button that bring people like him to justice. So, one last question and I'll let you rest for the night. Do you have any idea at all who your assailant is?"

"No I'm sorry I don't. I sensed the whole time that I knew him but I don't know why. There was just something really familiar about his voice even though it was a whisper...oh yes, and he definitely wore Old

Spice after shave. I remember smelling that every time he leaned over to whisper in my ear. And other than the button, that's it. Sorry! But I do wonder why he kept saying that I wanted him to do this, it was just strange."

"Oh don't be sorry sweetie, you have helped me immensely and I can only hope that I'm able to bring this guy to justice and send him to jail for the rest of his life for what he's done to you. I promise I won't give up until I get him for you."

We said our goodbyes and I let her rest for the night. Rest she deserved so very much.

27

The town was abuzz over the latest incident and the fear factor began to rise again. Things had really quieted down when the coach was arrested and no new cases appeared for those weeks he was in jail, but now with him still incarcerated and a new crime committed, everyone again began to doubt that he was really the murderer.

Lieutenant Franklin and his fellow detectives were devastated to see another crime happen but happy that Rhonda was not killed and also happy that they now had a few new clues to go on. Namely the blue long-sleeved shirt with a missing button and the smell of Old Spice after shave on the killer. He had instructed Rhonda not to mention those two things to anyone.

The lieutenant immediately began revisiting the entire male population in town to find out where they were. He knew the killer would be shocked to find out that Rhonda had survived, so he wanted to witness that immediate reaction when they were told.

To his surprise he ended up with the same few people who didn't have alibis for themselves in the other crimes. Brad Townsend, who was in the bleachers that day left to go to his studio for a few hours before heading over to Becky's house for dinner; Randy Bigby, was over at Stephanie's house for dinner but left to run to his apartment to freshen up and change clothes and fell asleep for about two hours; and Bob Thomas, Fran and Becky's dad was again down at the bank doing paperwork before he too had to be home for dinner. Neither of the three could come up with any kind of alibi since they were all alone.

The biggest reaction to Rhonda still being alive came from Randy who turned sheepishly white when he heard the news. Now in his defense he hadn't heard anything about Rhonda even being attacked so he may have reacted more to that than to the news of her still being alive. Brad had already heard from Becky about the attack so he seemed overjoyed that she had survived and the same with Bob Thomas, overjoyed that another girl hadn't been killed. But, in meeting with all three he definitely picked up on the Old Spice scent when talking with Mr. Thomas, so he shifted to the front of the list in the lieutenants eyes.

His team went back over the crime scene at the coach's house and turned up two cigarette butts, one outside behind those bushes that Rhonda suspected her assailant hid behind and the other on the porch. Both were the same brand and happened to be the brand that Brad smoked. They also found the same brand cigarette butt behind the bleachers and Brad was there that day also. So he too was beginning to look like a prime suspect.

The lieutenant felt like the blue shirt was his best clue so he decided to visit them one by one and see if he could find that shirt.

Going to the Thomas house first, he found that Mr. Thomas wasn't at home but his wife gladly answered a few questions and hesitantly agreed to let him look around. He looked through Mr. Thomas's clothes closet where all his shirts were neatly hung but there were no blue shirts. The lieutenant complimented her on the nice arrangement of shirts and she said her husband was an executive and always wanted to look his best so he had all his shirts done at the local cleaners next to the bank.

He stopped by Randy's apartment and after about a half hour of questions and answers he asked Randy if he would object to him looking around his apartment and Randy agreed. Randy had all of his shirts hanging in his bedroom closet and although he had two light blue shirts, one was short sleeve and the other had both buttons.

In visiting Brad's studio he went through the same line of questioning and Brad again agreed to let him look anywhere he wanted in the studio or his apartment upstairs. He found no light blue shirts at all in the closet or any drawers, which didn't surprise him too much because Brad was not a dress shirt kind of guy; he usually always wore polo shirts or button down golf shirts.

A day or two passed and some results were coming back from the lab regarding DNA on the cigarette butts and a very slight shoe impression that they found at the scene. The DNA found on the cigarettes was a definite match for Brad and the imprint was in fact the same boot imprint found at the scene of the Margy McNichol murder, the boots that had been found behind the coach's shed.

The lieutenant decided to visit all three of them again for another talk.

His first stop was over at the coach's house to get those boots and to his surprise they were gone. They weren't in the shed or behind it and were nowhere to be found, so that clue had disappeared.

On his way over to Brad's studio he happened to take a really good look at the cigarette butts and noticed that they were all in the same condition as the ones before, snuffed out by hand, not foot. So, as before, he suspected that maybe they had been planted there to point towards Brad, but who would know that Brad was in the bleachers that day except those people that were there, namely Randy and Bob Thomas.

He decided to swing by the bank and talk to Mr. Thomas first.

Arriving at the bank he glanced over and noticed the dry cleaning shop next to the bank that Mrs. Thomas had mentioned, so he decided to see if maybe there were some shirts there under the Thomas name.

He showed the owner his badge and he promptly retrieved a plastic covered group of hangers with newly cleaned and pressed shirts. Lieutenant Franklin could see right away that there were three yellow, two white and four blue shirts. He went right to the blue ones and one by one looked at the shirt sleeves and there it was, the second shirt in the group was a long sleeve light blue dress shirt with a missing button on the sleeve.

He immediately confiscated the entire lot of shirts and took them back to the precinct to see if the buttons matched the one Rhonda had given him.

The button was an exact match to the ones on the shirt and it was clearly evident when examining the shirt that the missing button on the sleeve had been pulled off and had not simply fallen off.

He felt now he had zeroed in on Bob Thomas as the attacker, having both the button-less blue shirt and the scent of Old Spice.

He was certain the entire Thomas family, as well as the community, would be devastated.

28

The evidence was there staring him in the face but he just knew it would turn out to be circumstantial evidence to the lawyers. Anyone could have a blue shirt with a button missing and hoards of men in the community used Old Spice after shave, so he knew he had to get more concrete evidence than what he had before he could confront Mr. Thomas or his family.

He sat in his office and laid out the four attacks, again finding that Bob Thomas was never home and never had anyone who could vouch for his whereabouts. He repeatedly said he was at the bank every time except the Margy McNichol murder when he said he was on a plane flying back from a business trip. The McNichol girl was thought to be murdered around 11pm so let's just see if in fact he was on a plane and what time it landed.

Calling the airline he had them trace all of their Chicago to Maryland flights and look for a Bob Thomas on that particular evening flight. They confirmed that he was in fact a passenger on Flight 727 from Chicago O'Hara Airport to BWI Airport in Baltimore that landed on schedule at 7:55pm. That would give him approximately three hours to get from the airport to Forest Hill and commit the murder.

The next thing he questioned was the incident in July when his daughter Fran was attacked by someone right outside of her home during a rain storm. It was just unusual to me that no one in the neighborhood saw anyone suspicious or running from the scene and it just so happened that Mr. Thomas was in the basement when the episode occurred. I wonder when he ran upstairs after hearing his daughter screaming if he was wet from being outside already?

Just as he was piecing things together and figuring out his next move, the telephone rang with some startling news. One of his partners was over to Brad's studio questioning him again and upon a search of his van found the missing duffel bag from the Rhonda Collins attack. He was bringing Brad in to the precinct for further questioning.

They arrived within moments, took Brad into the holding room for questioning, and brought the bag into the lieutenant. Searching through the bag he found Rhonda's old cheerleading outfit that she had on the day of the practice along with her undergarments and a makeup kit. It was clearly Rhonda's gym bag.

He entered the dimly lit room alone and sat down across from Brad.

"So what's the scoop Brad?"

"Lieutenant I know nothing about that bag in the back of my van. I tell you, just like before I'm being set up by someone. My van is always parked in back of the studio and it would be easy for someone to come along and just toss something into it."

"Maybe you should keep it locked from now on," said the lieutenant.

"Believe me I will. You've got to believe me though. After I left the school that day I went straight home to freshen up and change clothes. I was there maybe an hour or so and then left to go over Becky's house for dinner. I had dinner with her family and left about nine-thirty or so and went straight home and turned in. I had to get up early the next morning to head up to Hunt Valley for a meeting with the mall people."

"Did Mr. Thomas have dinner with all of you?"

"Yes but he got there a little late. We had just started dinner about six-thirty when he came in and said he just got tied up at the bank and hit a lot of traffic on the way home."

"Do you happen to remember what color shirt he was wearing when he came home?"

"Sure, a blue dress shirt with a red striped tie. I guess as a photographer I always notice what people are wearing and how they look. Why?"

"Oh just curious whether he was dressed for work or dressed casual, that's all. Look Brad, I'm going to take your word at this point that you didn't know anything about the bag because I know someone tried to set you up before, but I tell you if we find your fingerprints on that bag or anything in it, I'll be right out to your place to place you under arrest. Understood?"

"Understood lieutenant! Other than the malls in the area to set up these shows, I'll always be around, I'm not going anywhere."

The lieutenant released him and called his fellow detectives together to plan their strategy.

"First of all I don't believe for one second that Brad Townsend had anything to do with that duffel bag just like he didn't have anything to do with the bag of bloody clothes in his studio. He's not stupid enough to keep key evidence like that just laying around for anyone to find. So let's steer ourselves away from him and more on Bob Thomas."

"What's your gut feeling on Thomas?" asked Inspector Wiley.

"You know Tom, I just don't know. I mean this guy is an established executive banker in this community, he has a wonderful wife and two lovely daughters, and a beautiful home, so why would anyone like that risk murdering these girls or better yet what would his motive be."

"He has no criminal record at all," Inspector Burton added. "He's forty-seven years old, a veteran of the Navy, and seems to be a fine upstanding citizen volunteering for many social affairs throughout the community."

"I know all that, but in a way that's the kind of guy who has a ton of hidden secrets that no one knows about. I remember a pool party I went to last year at the Thomas house right after the Roxanne Willowby murder and he was quite the ladies man with the young girls. I mean he cooked up everything on the grill and was quite the host but he spent most of his time with the young girls; just seemed like he had his eyes on them most of the evening."

"But didn't his own daughter get attacked in front of her house?" asked George Burton.

"Yes, but you know I think that was a planned coy to lead everyone astray. I mean he has two beautiful daughters and all their girlfriends are getting attack yet nothing happens to them. And when something does happen to Fran it is in front of her house for a few seconds and she is unharmed."

"Brad Townsend said that Thomas was wearing a blue dress shirt when he showed up at the house late for dinner that night. And I located his blue shirts at the cleaners today and one of them has a missing button on the right sleeve just like Rhonda said. I really think he's our man," stated Lieutenant Franklin.

Just then Police Chief Dawson entered the room and approached the three of them.

"We need to make a decision on Coach Bannister," he said. "It's been a few days since the Collins girl was attacked and his lawyers are asking for him to be released."

"We still have a ton of evidence pointing his way but under the circumstances I guess we have to release him. If he is our killer than this had to be a copycat attack because obviously he was in jail when it happened," stated the lieutenant.

They all agreed that they couldn't formally charge the coach since this attack has placed a load of doubt on his case. They filled in the Chief on the rest of their conclusions regarding Bob Thomas and agreed to bring him in for questioning.

29

Bob Thomas came into the precinct full of rage and fit to tied. He was not a happy man!

"Lieutenant Franklin this is absurd. I can't believe you are calling me into here with the suspicions that I had anything to do with the murders of these young girls. I have two daughters their age and they are best friends with all of these young women, how could you think I could possibly have anything to do with their murders?" Mr. Thomas snapped at the lieutenant as he entered the interrogation room.

"Please have a seat Mr. Thomas and I'll be glad to explain our intentions here."

"Do I need a lawyer?"

"No sir not at this point you don't, but please just have a seat and let's talk about this," said Lieutenant Franklin as he pulled out a chair for him.

Bob Thomas grudgingly pulled the chair over towards himself and sat down silently placing his folded hands on the table in front of him. The lieutenant sat down across from him offering him something to drink but was refused.

"Mr. Thomas, the reason we called you in here today is to straighten out a few details that have surfaced in our running investigation. As I've said all along, we have to filter every minute detail that we uncover to either eliminate or substantiate all the possibilities. That's how we solve a case, trial and error. So...today I need to find out a few things regarding you. First of all, we keep coming back to you, along with a few other people, who have no alibis or witnesses to their whereabouts for each of the four attacks. You say you were at your bank for all of them except the Margy McNichol murder which you say you were flying home from Chicago."

"That's true lieutenant in every case. I am the executive officer of the local bank and responsible for a lot of peoples' money in this community. A lot of times I can't get everything accomplished in one day therefore I put in a lot of extra hours at the bank making sure things run smoothly. It's just part of my job."

"I know that Bob and I appreciate what you do for all of us in this community. As you know I myself have several accounts with your bank and can only imagine how much responsibility comes with that job, but let's talk about the plane flight from Chicago. I checked with the airline and found that Flight 727 from Chicago to BWI landed on time at 7:55pm. That would put you home at about 9pm or so and your wife said you arrived at about 11:45pm that night. Now what could have possibly taken you almost four hours to get home from the airport?"

"Well I don't exactly remember, uh let me see," said Mr. Thomas as he stuttered through the answer. "Well I went over and got my car out of the hourly parking garage and then stopped to get gas. Oh yes, and then I got something to eat. You know they don't feed you on those planes anymore."

"So we can obviously get someone at the restaurant where you ate to vouch for you being there? Say a waitress or cashier or a customer?"

"No I just slipped into a fast food drive-thru lane, ah Burger King I think it was...yes, Burger King because I got a Whopper with cheese and onion rings, and then I pulled into a spot and sat there eating it."

"For three hours?"

"No not for three hours. Let me see...I can't remember everything lieutenant. My wife must be mistaken; I couldn't have taken that long to get home!"

"Well we'll check back with her and see what she says. Now, the next question Mr. Thomas has to do with one of your blue dress shirts. I looked at one of your shirts that you wore last week and see that a button has been pulled off the sleeve. Can you tell me how that happened?"

"I don't really recall wearing a blue shirt last week lieutenant; I think I wore white shirts to the office all week long. I usually always wear a white shirt when I'm meeting with customers, it's much more formal."

"Okay, let me refresh your memory sir. The day that I came to the school and met you in the bleachers at cheerleading practice, remember that? You were there with your daughter Fran, and Brad Townsend was there, and Randy Bigby. Remember that?"

"Yes I remember that day."

"Well sir you had on a blue dress shirt with a red tie. And you were wearing that same shirt when you arrived at home for dinner with your family and Brad. By the way, why were you so late to dinner that evening?"

"Just got caught up in paperwork and then hit a lot of traffic on the way home. What's with all these questions lieutenant, am I suspected of these crimes?"

"As I said before we're just trying to piece together everybody's whereabouts and what they were doing at the time of the crimes. You are no more a suspect than anyone else except for the fact that most people have alibis and you don't, that's all. Now back to the question of the blue shirt."

"I don't know lieutenant, if you say I was wearing a blue dress shirt that day then I guess I was. As far as the button, I think I remember snagging it on the bleachers when I was at the practice that day."

"Okay good enough Mr. Thomas, I appreciate you taking the time to come down here and answer a few questions and you're certainly free to go anytime you want."

"You're welcome. I'm sorry I was so snippety when I first got here but I just have the feeling you're questioning me an awful lot, but maybe you're questioning everyone a whole lot. I understand you have a job to do just like I do at the bank and I appreciate that," he said as he held out his hand to the lieutenant.

They shook hands and Lieutenant Franklin reiterated that they had many people they were continuing to question and he should not plan any trips out of the general area in the foreseeable future.

Bob Thomas left the precinct feeling as if he was a guilty man in their eyes and close to being charged with the crimes. It would be very difficult for him to continue in his daily functions knowing the police were looking over his shoulder every minute. He wasn't the type of person to easily forget the accusations and pressure.

30

Becky was so excited about the coming week and weekend that she could hardly control herself. First she had two appointments during the week, one to get fitted for her bridesmaid gown and the other to help Fran and her mom pick out invitations and favors for the upcoming wedding. It was so exciting thinking about the wedding and dreaming of the day it would be her turn to pick everything out and walk down the aisle. Second it was the weekend of the first mall show with Brad and she shivered with excitement just thinking about being with him all weekend, how exciting!

She had classes in the mid morning so she slipped by the studio on her way to see him before he left for the mall to make final arrangements. As she walked up he was loading equipment into the back of his van.

"Hey Becky I didn't expect to see you today," Brad said with a joyful smile on his face.

"I know, I just wanted to stop by on my way to class and wish you well today. I knew I wouldn't see you later and I knew I couldn't stand not getting my daily kiss," she said with a sexy smile and wink of the eye as she walked towards him.

She was such a beautiful and sexy girl and knew just how to handle herself to drive the opposite sex wild with anticipation. Her long blonde hair fell over her black blouse that was neatly tucked into her white short, short mini skirt revealing her long tanned legs.

Brad dropped what he was doing and met her with open arms.

"Wow, you sure know how to leave a guy with a lasting memory," he said as he scanned her figure from head to toe and wrapped his arms around her waist.

They kissed a long passionate kiss and both pulled back with a smile of satisfaction on their face.

"Now try not to think about me while you're slaving away at the mall all day," she said as she walked away glancing over her shoulder with a smirk on her face.

"And you have fun in class today and also tonight with your gown fitting. By the way, have you told your parents that I'll be your escort at the wedding?"

"Not yet, but I will this week. I want to prepare them slowly."

They both continued to stare at each other as she headed down the road and the short walk to class.

She only had one class today, it was her easiest day of the week and she was glad because she knew her mind was just not into listening to lectures and taking notes, so when class was over early she bolted out of the room. Fran was supposed to pick her up at school to head downtown but she gave her a quick call on her cell phone to let her know she was finished class early and wanted to walk home and change before they left. Fran said she was running an errand and and would meet her at the house.

She arrived home and went straight to her upstairs bedroom knowing that Fran would be home at any minute to pick her up so they could meet their mom at the shop. She had no sooner got upstairs when she heard the front door open and Fran yelled up to her that she was there and would wait in the kitchen.

She didn't have much to do, she just didn't want to wear the white mini skirt downtown, that was just for Brad's benefit as she smiled taking it off and thinking of the smile on his face as he looked at her. She shimmied it off, grabbed her purse, and walked into Fran's bedroom to pick out a pair of her slacks to put on when she heard a scream from downstairs.

She raced to her door only to hear Fran's scream become muffled and things being knocked over from the apparent struggle that was taking place in the kitchen. Immediately she knew Fran was being attacked and the intruder obviously didn't know she was upstairs.

She hastily buttoned her pants and went straight for her cell phone to call for help. She knew she couldn't do anything herself so she dialed 911 and told them to send the police immediately. Just as she clicked the phone off she could hear the struggle and muffled screams coming up the stairs as she sensed the intruder was dragging her up the stairs to the bedroom. She raced for the closet and closed the shuttered doors to hide as she got back on her phone and called the lieutenants number. Just as he answered the bedroom door burst open and she clicked the phone off.

Becky was in shock. She peered out of the shutters of the closed closet door and saw Fran being pushed through the doorway and onto the bed by her father.

"Dad what are you doing?" she screamed as tears of fright streamed down her face.

"I am so sorry sweetie, you're the last person in the world I would want to hurt but I just have to. They're after me sweetie, they think I killed all those girls and I just can't let that happen," her dad said as tears also streamed down his eyes. "I just can't go to jail for those crimes, I'm a well respected banker and I just can't help it if I have this uncontrollable passion for all those beautiful girls. They just kept tempting me and tempting me until I couldn't take it anymore."

"Daddy it's me Fran, your daughter. Please don't hurt me."

"I'm so sorry sweetie, I don't want to, but I have to do something to get the police off my back. I have to make them think it is someone else committing these crimes or I'll go to jail. You have to understand Franie...I just have to."

Becky looked out from the closet in disbelief and horror-stricken as she listened to her dad and watched the fear grip her sister's face.

"I'm so sorry sweetie," he repeated as he got on the bed and straddled on top of her taping her flailing hands together. "I'm sorry Franie," he said again as he put a piece of tape over her mouth and began to rip off her blouse and bra.

Becky couldn't wait any longer. She knew the police were probably on their way and she feared for

Fran's life. She knew he might act quickly to get it over with so she had to do something.

With tears streaming down his face and continuous pleas for her forgiveness he moved down her body and began to remove her skirt and panties. It was then that Becky threw open the closet doors and lunged at the bed.

Her dad was completely taken by surprise and as big as he was the force of Becky's body knocked him off of Fran and onto the floor.

Becky went right to her sister and ripped the tape off of her mouth and began getting her hands free.

"Becky, what are you doing here? Where did you come from?" he said with an astonished look on his tear filled face.

"Stay away from us Dad," she yelled as her and Fran hugged closely together on the bed.

"I'm so sorry girls, please forgive me, but your dad is just sick with grief and ashamed of what he has done. All those beautiful girls were just too much for me. They just always teased me and flaunted themselves at me and I just couldn't help myself. I'm only human you know. You've both got to understand why I did those awful things and why I've got to do this. They would never think I'd do anything to my own daughters," he said as his face became rigid and he stood up beside the bed. "It's either that high school coach or that Brad Townsend that the police will go after, I'll make sure of that. I just hate seeing him around you Becky."

"Dad stop it, just stop it right now," Fran screamed as their father again approached the bed with his two shivering daughters in it.

It was two of them but even so they were no match for his size and strength. He jumped on the bed forcing the embracing girls under him as he straddled both of them. They were both the same size, small and petite, so no match for him at all.

They both began to kick and punch at him trying to force him off balance and back onto the floor. He grabbed Becky's blouse and ripped it off screaming at them to stop resisting him that he just had to do this or he'd go to jail forever.

It was then that they heard the front door downstairs thrust open and they both began screaming in unison. Within seconds Lieutenant Franklin and three police officers burst into the bedroom with guns drawn. They were so quick that they caught Bob Thomas almost be surprise as he sat on the bed staring at them with tears still streaming down his face.

"I'm so sorry, I'm just so sorry," he kept repeating as the officers confronted him. "I just had to prove to you that it wasn't me. I just couldn't do something like that lieutenant."

The officers pulled him off the bed and wrapped his arms behind him as they handcuffed him. Tears continued to run down his face as they led him out of the bedroom.

"I'm so sorry girls, I do love you both so very much," he said as he looked back at them with tear-soaked eyes. "Please understand why I had to do this…you understand don't you girls?"

The two girls were in each other's tight grip as their shivering bodies were entwined with each other. The lieutenant reached down and pulled a sheet up over their half-naked bodies as he sat on the edge of the bed and leaning over hugged them both.

"It's all over girls, it's all over."

They could still hear their dad being led down the stairs and out the front door.

"It wasn't me, really it wasn't me. It was Brad Townsend. You have a lot of evidence pointing towards him right? It was him, not me. And you tell him to stay away from my daughter Becky. He's a murderer."

Their crying continued as they never stopped hugging each other.

The lieutenant called for an ambulance as he again leaned over and embraced both of the shivering girls who had just been through a horrific ordeal to say the least.

He knew as he left their house that day that it would be a very long time before the family as well as the community would heal from the tragic events that had taken place in this small community of young girls.

He also knew that all he wanted to do was to get home to his two daughters tonight and give them both a big hug.

Please visit his online bookstore for a review of all of the G. Lusby books now available.

www.lulu.com/GLusbyBooks

Serial
G. Lusby

Made in the USA
Lexington, KY
30 March 2015